What the critics are saying…

About *The Angelini: Skye's Trail*

"Once again, *Jory Strong* crafts a strong paranormal romance with a leading heroine who can kick some serious butt. Skye is not a woman to mess with… Though this story has a thrilling plot and an equally thrilling romance with two alpha males, it is Skye who is the heart and soul of this story. Kudos to *Ms. Strong* for creating such an unforgettable story!..." ~ *Sarah, A Romance Review*

"This book was delicious and sensually erotic. The relationship and consequent friction between these three characters was spine tingling." ~ *Dianne Nogueras, eCata Romance*

About *Crime Tells: Lyric's Cop*

"*Crime Tells: Lyric's Cop* has it ALL! Strong characters, witty dialogue, blazing sex scenes, and a great plot combine to make this a page turner that will stay in your reread files for a long time." ~ *Trang Noire, Just Erotic Romance Reviews*

"*Lyric's Cop* is a well written, fast-paced, and very erotic mystery story. The erotic tension between Kieran and Lyric is scorching, while the mystery surrounding the dogs is heart-wrenching while at the same time very interesting..." ~ *Sarah W, Fallen Angel Reviews*

JORY STRONG

ELLORA'S CAVE
ROMANTICA PUBLISHING

An Ellora's Cave Romantica Publication

www.ellorascave.com

Calista's Men

ISBN # 1419953117
ALL RIGHTS RESERVED.
Calista's Men Copyright© 2005 Jory Strong
Edited by: Sue-Ellen Gower
Cover art by: Syneca

Electronic book Publication: June, 2005
Trade paperback Publication: December, 2005

Excerpt from *Cady's Cowboy* Copyright © Jory Strong, 2005

Warning:

The following material contains graphic sexual content meant for mature readers. *Calista's Men* has been rated *E-rotic* by a minimum of three independent reviewers.

Ellora's Cave Publishing offers three levels of Romantica™ reading entertainment: S (S-ensuous), E (E-rotic), and X (X-treme).

S-*ensuous* love scenes are explicit and leave nothing to the imagination.

E-*rotic* love scenes are explicit, leave nothing to the imagination, and are high in volume per the overall word count. In addition, some E-rated titles might contain fantasy material that some readers find objectionable, such as bondage, submission, same sex encounters, forced seductions, etc. E-rated titles are the most graphic titles we carry; it is common, for instance, for an author to use words such as "fucking", "cock", "pussy", etc., within their work of literature.

X-*treme* titles differ from E-rated titles only in plot premise and storyline execution. Unlike E rated titles, stories designated with the letter X tend to contain controversial subject matter not for the faint of heart.

Also by Jory Strong:

Calista's Men

Crime Tells

Trademarks Acknowledgement

The author acknowledges the trademarked status and trademark owners of the following wordmarks mentioned in this work of fiction:

Starbucks: Starbucks U.S. Brands Corporation

Liar's Dice: MTGR Corporation DBA Murphy-Goode Estate Winery

Beetle: Volkswagen Aktiengesellschaft

Jeep Wrangler: DaimlerChrysler Corporation

Jockey: Jockey International, Inc.

Tinkertoys: Playskool, Inc.

Lego: Kirkbi AG

Diet Coke: The Coca-Cola Company

Mustang: Ford Motor Company

Play-doh: Hasbro, Inc.

Noah's: Noah's New York Bagels, Inc.

Scrabble: Production and Marketing Corporation, The

Yahtzee: E. S. Lowe Company, INC.

Lexus: Toyota Motor Sales, U.S.A., Inc.

Chapter One

Calista Burke wanted to pinch herself...that is, in the seconds when her stomach wasn't threatening to embarrass her by heaving the remains of her stop at Starbucks onto the Crime Tells' carpet.

She'd done it. She'd landed the job—or more accurately, she'd landed a chance to try the job.

She wanted to jump up and down, to give Tyler Keane and Lyric and Erin Montgomery huge hugs for all the time they'd spent telling her how they solved cases, and more importantly, all the hours they'd spent teaching her how to play poker.

That had been part of the interview.

Calista wiped damp palms against her jeans. She hadn't won a single hand, except when Bulldog Montgomery folded, but she must have done okay. Whatever he'd been looking for, he must have found, because both Lyric and Erin said their grandfather didn't take on a case or let someone work for him until he'd challenged that person to a game of cards so he could see what they were made of.

She grinned. She'd spent so much time around the Montgomerys and Maguires that she didn't even blink anymore when someone pulled out a deck of cards or cup of dice in order to decide who was going to make a run for Starbucks or pay for a take-out order—or, when it was just the girls, who was going to be the one to spill their guts and share a personal tidbit of information, especially a sexual one. Gambling was in their blood. And it all started with Bulldog.

Until he'd semi-retired and started Crime Tells, Bulldog Montgomery was one of the most sought after detectives in the gambling business. Even now, he was still called in to consult, though he just as often sent one of his grandchildren to work the case, and he didn't limit himself to gambling cases anymore. He took on a wide variety of cases in Northern California, anything that grabbed his interest or seemed like something his grandchildren or the other detectives working for him would enjoy handling.

Calista grinned. *And now I'm not only one of them, but I'm about to get my first case.*

Her heart did a little hippity-hop in her chest. Never in a million years would she have guessed that when her brother, Kieran, finally fell in love and married Lyric Montgomery, it would change her life too.

But then, no one could spend time around Lyric without developing a little streak of adventure, without at least considering the possibility of "going for the gusto" as Lyric loved to counsel.

Calista looked around her. Well, this was part one of her great adventure. The next part was a little harder—actually *being* a detective instead of what she'd been since graduating from college, a kindergarten teacher.

The Burke family had always run heavy on police, firemen and schoolteachers—with the men getting the first two professions and the women ending up in the classroom. Calista straightened her shoulders. Well, now it was time to break out of that mold. Grinning, she picked up the phone to dial her sister-in-law, but before she could punch in the second number, a woman walked into the office.

A ball of nerves settled in Calista's stomach. *Think the first day of school with a class full of scared kids and neurotic parents. Dealing with a client will be a piece of cake compared to that.* She settled the phone back in its cradle and smiled at the woman. "I'm Calista Burke. You're here to see Bulldog?"

The woman frowned slightly, checking her expensive watch before holding out a manicured hand with two gem-laden rings and a diamond tennis bracelet. "Yes. I'm Sarah Winston. He's expecting me."

Calista shook the extended hand. "I'll tell him you're here."

She could have used the speakerphone, but instead she walked over and knocked on Bulldog's door, giving herself a few seconds to try and unwind the tight knot in her stomach.

Inside Bulldog's office, a dog barked followed by Bulldog's gruff, "Come in."

Calista stepped inside, smiling at the fierce man with the dappled dachshund on his lap. The dog was Lyric's doing. In fact, almost everyone in the Montgomery and Maguire families, plus a multitude of friends, had ended up with miniature dachshunds thanks to the case that had brought Kieran and Lyric together—the case that had started when someone mugged Calista's own grandmother and stole her three dogs.

"Sarah Winston's here," Calista mouthed since Bulldog was on the phone. He gave her a nod and a hand signal to come ahead into the office. She retreated just long enough to motion Sarah in and to retrieve a small notebook before taking a seat.

Calista's thoughts danced with speculation as to what kind of problem Sarah Winston might have. The woman's thick Southern drawl made her think that she was either a recent transplant to California or was here visiting.

Bulldog hung up the phone and rose far enough to shake Sarah's hand, saying, "My condolences for your loss," before dropping back into his seat.

The client nodded slightly. "I appreciate you taking this case on. I know it's not the kind of thing you usually deal with."

Bulldog shrugged. "Greg and I go way back."

A slight smile warmed Sarah's features. "Yes, all the way to college, I believe. My brother still claims those were the best years of his life."

Bulldog chuckled and settled more comfortably in his chair. Sarah's eyes skittered to Calista and he said, "You've met Calista. She'll be lead detective on this, though all of us will work on the case if necessary. Why don't you go ahead and give us an overview. Calista and I will jump in if we have any questions."

Sarah hesitated, her shoulders slumping for just an instant before her backbone stiffened into an amazingly straight line. "My daughter died last week. The cause of death is listed as an accidental death while under the influence of drugs." She paused, as if needing to push more steel into her spine before continuing. "I insisted that an autopsy be done. The coroner confirmed the presence of ecstasy in Jessica's system along with alcohol and another drug. He also discovered my daughter had given birth sometime in the recent past. I want to know what happened to my grandchild."

Bulldog nodded. "That's understandable. I assume the police checked your daughter's home?"

"Yes. They found no evidence a baby had ever been there. For that matter, they found nothing to indicate my daughter was expecting. And quite frankly, they weren't interested in investigating further. The officer in charge said he'd done a routine check of hospital delivery records and hadn't found my daughter's name listed. He implied that since I hadn't even known she was pregnant, she'd either had a late-term abortion or had given the child up for adoption. Either way, there was no evidence to suggest a crime, and the department lacks the resources to pursue it further. He suggested I hire a private investigator."

Bulldog nodded again before his attention shifted to Calista. Her muscles tensed at the silent handoff of authority. Her grip tightened on her pencil and she tried to think like Lyric or Erin or Cady would think—and went blank.

She almost panicked. But years of being a teacher saved her.

One small step at a time. One question and answer building on the last one.

She took a steadying breath. "You said your daughter's death was ruled accidental. What happened?"

"She was attending a party and fell from a tenth-floor balcony. When the police arrived at the scene they found an assortment of drugs in the apartment where the party was being held."

Calista bit her bottom lip. She felt like she was poking in an open wound, even though nothing in Sarah's demeanor made it obvious. "Were there witnesses?"

Sarah gave a quick, negative shake of her head. "Apparently my daughter had gone into one of the bedrooms in order to use the bathroom. The balcony was off the bedroom." Her face hardened, turning into an ivory mask. "She did not commit suicide, if that's what you're thinking. The police found nothing to indicate anything other than an accident. I talked to Jessica a couple of weeks ago and she was in excellent spirits. She'd just received a bonus for a job she had completed. She was excited about renting a house in Hawaii and spending some time there."

"What kind of work did your daughter do?"

"I'm not sure. I'll be frank with you, my daughter and I have been estranged since she moved to California. Her phone call was the first time I've talked to her in the last year and a half."

"Do you have a recent picture?"

"Of course." She opened her handbag and pulled out a folded manila envelope and handed it to Calista. "Inside you'll also find the key to her apartment along with the manager's name and phone number. I've made arrangements for him to dispose of Jessica's belongings as soon as you contact him and tell him you no longer need to view the apartment."

Calista opened the envelope. Along with the key and photo were copies of the police and autopsy reports, complete with Jessica's address, social security number and birth date.

The last piece of information struck at Calista's core. Jessica Rose Winston would have been twenty-four in another two months.

"Besides the bonus and the trip to Hawaii, did Jessica mention anything else?"

For the first time, Sarah looked away. "No. Despite the fact she was in high spirits, it wasn't a friendly call. Her move to California wasn't the beginning of our estrangement. My husband and I have always felt Jessica didn't live up to her potential. She was an incredibly bright girl, but quite frankly, she was...she always...settled, when with a little effort she could have excelled. Her call was more of a call to let us know we'd always been wrong about her rather than an attempt at reconciliation. She wouldn't even give me an address or a phone number."

Sarah's hand tightened on her purse until her knuckles went white. When she released her grip, her shoulders dipped for a split second. Without a word she opened her purse and pulled out another envelope and handed it to Calista. Inside was a bank statement in the name of Lindsey Smyth, with a Nevada address and a balance of over a hundred thousand dollars.

"I found the statement in Jessica's apartment, with some brochures about Hawaii."

Calista frowned. "Did you show it to the police?"

"No." Sarah's eyes met hers. "The police have already demonstrated they're not interested in pursuing this matter further. At this point, I just want to find out what happened to my grandchild."

Calista nodded. "I can understand that. Where can I reach you?"

Sarah dug into the purse on her lap one more time and pulled out an embossed card—a calling card, not a business card. "I'll be returning to Georgia tonight. I'm accompanying my daughter's body back to Atlanta." She paused before adding, "I'm sorry I left this so late, but I wasn't sure whether or not I wanted to pursue it further until after I'd checked out of the hotel and finalized the arrangements for my daughter."

Calista shot a quick glance at Bulldog. "We'll keep you updated on our progress."

Sarah rose from her chair. "I would certainly appreciate that. If Mr. Winston should answer the telephone, please don't discuss this matter with him. He's in poor health. I would prefer he not be involved at this point. Perhaps later…"

"Of course," Bulldog said, entering the conversation as he stood and offered his hand again. "I'm sorry for your loss, Sarah. We'll do what we can."

Sarah smiled slightly and for the first time Calista could see the weary heartbreak in her face. "Thank you," she said, turning to shake Calista's hand before leaving the office, her spine straight, her footsteps never faltering.

When the outer office door closed, Bulldog shook his head and said, "Times like these make me realize how lucky I was with my children and grandchildren."

For a moment Calista's thoughts returned to the classroom, to the children she'd taught. By the time they'd reached kindergarten, they were no longer blank pages, but their lives still held so much hope, so much promise—like wonderful novels yet to be written. She hated knowing some of the stories turned into tragedies.

Bulldog moved around his desk, pausing just long enough to straighten a stack of poker chips before reaching for a leash and attaching it to the now animated dachshund's collar. "Time to call it a night," he said. "If I know Lyric and Tyler, they're waiting for a call from you and an excuse to celebrate. I think your first case is good cause for that. Just don't let them talk you into playing Liar's Dice for money. They're both sharks."

Calista laughed and followed him out, anticipation bubbling through her. She'd celebrate with her friends tonight and tomorrow she'd tackle her first case.

Chapter Two

Detective Dante Giancotti almost halted at the bar entrance and returned to his car. He wasn't in the mood for fawning, easy women tonight. Hell, he wasn't even good company for himself.

Fuck. He hated being on administrative leave. Hated the fact it was dragging out because the perp he'd shot and killed was the seventeen-year-old son of a wealthy family. A family that couldn't believe their angel, in the company of his older brother and a friend, had offed a drug dealer named P.J. Henderson before turning the gun toward Dante, forcing him to shoot.

Christ. What a fucking nightmare.

The Mitchells' money and their big-name lawyer had turned it into a trial-by-newspaper, with Dante the bad guy and the kid being portrayed as a saintly son who'd been outraged and gone after Henderson because someone had bought a date-rape-rave-party-cocktail from the dealer and slipped it to the Mitchell kid's girlfriend.

Son of a bitch. They could paint it any way they wanted it. But that's not how it had looked to him. Yeah, he'd come on the scene unexpectedly and had needed to act fast, but he hadn't seen passion. He'd seen murder.

Fucking liberals couldn't seem to get a grip on the fact that a kid with a gun could be every bit as coldly motivated as a hit man.

And it didn't help that it'd been Dante's third shooting since he joined the San Francisco police department. The fifth since he'd gotten out of the police academy. What everyone, including Internal Affairs, seemed to forget was that two of them were "suicide by cop" scenarios. Christ, it still burned to be used like that, to be forced into a situation where he had to draw his gun and take a life because someone with a death wish couldn't bring themselves to actually commit suicide.

Now he was being painted as some trigger-happy vigilante of a cop running around shooting the citizens. Shit. Maybe Benito was right, maybe it was time to quit the force. Who needed this?

Dante scowled and pressed forward. His eyes quickly adjusting to the dim lighting in the bar and finding his twin at their usual table. Alone. For now, anyway.

Not that Dante didn't get his share of women—there were plenty of them who liked to spread their legs for cops—but his brother's midnight-black ponytail and diamond earring were fuck-magnets. Dante's cock stirred and his mood lightened slightly. Hell, maybe a good lay was what he needed to take the edge off.

He'd enjoyed any number of the women who'd gone for Benito. The same was true in reverse, though it was a little riskier.

Women talked. To each other. To the next cop they got in the sack with. And before he knew it, the guys in the locker room were like adolescents who'd just seen their first porn movie. He couldn't shut them up.

But that wasn't the worst of it. The worst of it was that sooner or later someone would suggest getting together and doing it to their girlfriend or some other girl they knew who was hot to have two men at once.

It didn't work that way for Dante. Or his brother.

Hell, some shrink could probably write a book on why he and Benito shared the same woman. He could write part of the book himself.

But it didn't change the fact. Didn't change the need.

His cock pulsed and stirred, warming to the idea now that he was thinking about it. Between his work and Benito's, it had been months since they'd found a willing woman.

Dante grimaced as he remembered the heavy, uncomfortable conversation that had followed the last time, after they'd finally dislodged the woman from Benito's house.

I want more than this, his brother had said, his arm making a sweeping gesture.

More? You've got extra bedrooms, a room with a pool table, a weight room, a hot tub and a TV room with a big-screen TV. What do you want that you don't have?

Have you ever wondered what it would be like with a woman we actually cared about? One who belonged just to us? One who wanted more from us than a good time and a great fuck story to tell her friends? A woman we could have together or separately? One who saw us as individuals who came as a package deal? One who was waiting for us at the end of the day?

No.

No?

I like them easy and I like to share them with you. End of story, Benito.

And they'd left it at that, though now Dante's gut tightened. Is that why they hadn't gotten together since?

His thoughts scrambled backward, looking for a conversation, a chance opportunity to take a woman home and share her. There wasn't one. Dante relaxed. It was just work. Different schedules, different cities…hell, these days it seemed like his brother spent more time in Nevada than California.

Benito stood when Dante got to the table, offering a handshake that slid into a hug. "Ready to turn in the badge yet?" he asked as they pulled apart.

Dante grunted and took a seat. "I'm tempted." And he realized he really was.

"Anytime, Dante, the company is half yours whether you put another dime into it or not. You know that. We could split the work up any way you want it. And I could really use your help managing the personal protection jobs." Benito grinned and shook his head. "Right now it's a hot status symbol to go into the chic bars and restaurants with bodyguards. It's good money, but not my interest."

Dante settled more comfortably in his chair. "How many guys have you got working security?"

Benito grimaced. "That's part of the problem, finding qualified guys and keeping them. At first they get a kick out of hanging around with stars and near-stars, but it gets old and boring pretty quick. If the money weren't so good…" He shrugged. "And some of the time the bodyguard gigs lead to real security work, state-of-the-art systems."

A waitress stopped by the table and took their drink orders, followed almost immediately by a big-breasted blonde with glossy red lips and a fuck-me-tonight come-on. Benito turned her down before Dante had even decided whether she was a possibility or not.

"A little quick there, bro," Dante said, his gut tightening again. "It's been a while."

Something flickered in Benito's eyes before he shrugged. "She didn't do it for me."

And uninvited, unwanted, their last conversation about women spread out like a dark, silent stain between them.

Fuck.

Dante looked away. He didn't want to deal with this right now. Hell, he didn't want to deal with it at all. Their twin-bond, the love they held for each other, their closeness had not only helped them survive to adulthood but to end up somewhere other than jail or the ghetto.

His heart lurched. Christ, to think something...a woman...would drive open a rift between them was almost unbearable.

Dante met his brother's gaze. Whatever was happening with Benito, he wanted it out on the table. "You've met someone?"

Benito's dark eyes, mirror images of his own, actually flashed with amusement momentarily, and then with surprise as his attention shifted to the bar entrance. "Not yet, but I'd like to."

Dante turned in his seat and his cock went from mildly interested to flat-out desperate, while at the same time his mind traveled from *oh yeah* at the sight of the dark-haired beauty to *oh fuck* when he saw who she came in with. "Shit."

The two women could almost be twins themselves except the one with the raven-black curls halfway down her back was just a little taller and oozed sensuousness while the one with the straight hair, the one who had Dante's cock pressing hard against his jeans, had an innocence about her that usually would have been more effective than a cold shower.

"You know her?" Benito asked, his cock thick and hard and straight as it strained to get past his waistband. He hadn't been with a woman since the last one he and Dante had taken together, hadn't thought to seek one out either alone or with his brother—not that the need wasn't there, but it had changed and deepened until he knew a parade of easy, forgettable women wouldn't give him what he craved.

He hadn't intended to pursue a woman tonight. He hadn't even planned on bringing up the subject of women again until this mess with the shooting was over. He'd planned only on trying to persuade his brother to take over part of the Giancotti Security operation.

His intentions changed the moment the dark-haired woman walked into the bar and his heart tripped into an unsteady beat while his cock rose to rigid attention. He couldn't make out her features clearly, but she looked delicate, soft, with gentle curves that made him think of intense sex—followed by a lingering warmth instead of the usual need to disentangle and distance himself. "You know her?" Benito repeated, his eyes moving to Dante and seeing the lust riding his twin.

"The one with the long curls is Lyric Montgomery. Now Burke. She's married to a vice cop."

Benito gave a slight shake of his head, confirming what Dante already knew. It was the woman with Lyric who had caught his brother's attention. "What about the other one?"

"I don't think I've seen her before." He shrugged. "But I don't spend a lot of time down here."

They watched as the two women found a table, then frowned identical frowns when a blond man sporting a ponytail just as long as Benito's joined them, receiving a hug and a kiss from both women before he sat down.

"I want to meet her," Benito said, hating the timing, hating that he had to push now when he'd been prepared to hold until Dante's head got clear about his career, hating that he risked opening a rift between them. But his gut, hell, his cock was screaming at him not to let the opportunity to meet this woman pass.

Dante gritted his teeth. Shit. Either way he was screwed. Benito would go over and introduce himself whether he went or not. "She's not what you usually go for," he said, already knowing it didn't matter. Hell, his own cock was aching for a chance at her.

Benito shrugged and rose from his seat. Cursing, Dante also stood.

Calista watched as the two men approached. God, they were gorgeous. Brothers, maybe twins, not identical but close enough. She recognized the one with the shorter hair, his face had been in the news lately. He might be a cop, but he had the dark Italian looks and confidence of a street-wise gangster. Dante something. She should remember it. He'd been a topic of conversation around her parents' dinner table. To a one, the men in her family agreed he'd done what a cop had to do and made a righteous kill. Too bad the perp had come from a moneyed, politically inclined family.

She shivered—the pictures hadn't done Dante justice. The man was a walking orgasm, a sexual animal that could give a woman a night she'd never forget. Or repeat. His hard eyes and hard face were warning enough. The only thing he was offering was his body, and only while it suited him.

Calista's eyes moved to the brother and a ball of heated anticipation settled low in her belly, sending a warm flush through her cunt. She'd always had a thing for men with long hair, and this one, with the soft eyes and the lips that promised unspeakable pleasure, had her praying they weren't zeroing in on Lyric. That would be a major bummer. Not that she wouldn't understand it, but…

She straightened her shoulders. This was her night, and if a couple of guys couldn't resist hitting on Lyric, then she was not going to get upset about it. She wasn't going to let it ruin her excitement about getting a chance to work a case for Crime Tells. She was not in a competition with Lyric. Any guy would want to do her sister-in-law. Of course, if they were stupid enough to try it, Kieran would convince them it wasn't a good idea. But…

"Oh shit," Lyric muttered, "Kieran is never going to believe I didn't have something to do with this."

"Not with your reputation," Tyler Keane agreed and Calista's attention shifted back to her companions.

"What?" she asked, her interest instantly piqued by the mischief dancing in Lyric's eyes. What had she ever done without Lyric in her life? Her sister-in-law was a walking catalyst for change.

"That's Dante Giancotti heading our way. I met him when I was helping Cady on her last case, well, the last one before she took off to Texas with Kix." Lyric grinned.

"Kieran was with me and I teased him with the prospect of introducing Dante to you."

Heat rushed to Calista's cheeks. She could just imagine how that had gone over. The men in her family tended to be overprotective, and that was a gross understatement. Calista shook her head. "Don't bother repeating what Big Brother said. I can guess."

Lyric actually snickered. "I won't have to. I'm sure he'll tell you himself when he gets here." Her eyes moved from the approaching Giancotti brothers to the exquisitely delicious Tyler, who'd been her childhood friend and who now worked as a police artist and as a consultant for Crime Tells. "But don't expect Kieran and me to stick around for long. Not with all this gorgeous male flesh present." Her eyebrows went up and down. "You know how your brother gets when he's around too much testosterone."

Calista was still laughing as Dante and his brother reached the table.

"Mind if we join you?" Benito asked after his brother and Lyric had made the introductions.

Lyric's laugh was pure mischief. "That'd be great, pull up a chair. We're celebrating. As of today, Calista is working for Crime Tells."

Heat swamped Calista when Benito and Dante took positions on either side of her, their thighs brushing and settling against hers, trapping her between their warm bodies and masculine scent. She knew without looking that her nipples were outlined against her shirt. A blush washed over her face, but there was nothing she could do short of crossing her arms over her chest, and that would be embarrassingly obvious.

"You're a private investigator?" Benito asked, his dark eyes and smooth voice curling around Calista's cunt like a warm hand. She squeezed her thighs together, the blush deepening as she felt her muscles sliding against theirs, as she saw the knowledge in Benito's eyes that he knew what the movement meant.

"I'm trying it out," Calista said, groaning inwardly at how pathetic she sounded. "I mean, I've been a kindergarten teacher since I got out of college. And I've enjoyed it. But now I want to try something different."

She exchanged glances with Lyric and had to hold back a grin. The idea to work for Crime Tells had come about one night when Calista was visiting her sister-in-law, complaining that the only men she met as a teacher were divorced fathers, married fathers and lecherous fathers.

Dante held back a groan. A fucking kindergarten teacher. It figured. Everything about her was soft and feminine. Christ. This was the last thing he needed, to get involved with another cop's sister, with a woman who'd probably freak out if the sex got rough.

A hard beat pulsed through his cock and Dante gritted his teeth. Not *if* the sex got rough, but *when*.

Fuck. When he and Benito were with the same woman, he could hold off the need to have her completely submissive, to thoroughly dominate her. The pleasure of sharing her with his brother was enough. But the craving was still there, burning side by side with the desire to take her while his brother fucked her.

Christ. Calista was all wrong—for him, for them. But even as Dante thought it, Benito rose from the table and drew Calista out to the dance floor for a slow song.

Dante's penis jerked, hungry to experience the pleasure of rubbing against Calista as his brother's cock was doing.

Chapter Three

Heaven. Everything about her was heaven, Benito thought as he held Calista, savoring the fit of their bodies, the way she melted into him, cuddling his erection and yet blushing slightly at the feel of it against her. She was exactly what he'd been hungering for.

There were a thousand things he wanted to know about her. But right here, right now, all he could think about was how wonderful she felt against his body. How much he wanted to take her home with him, to get her underneath him and make love to her.

He was ready for love. He was ready to open his heart and his life to it. To love someone besides his brother.

And that was a first.

Their childhood hadn't exactly lent itself to tender feelings. A drug addicted, prostitute mother who'd tried to sell her sons for dope money. A long string of social workers who'd seen so much that they'd burned out long before Dante and Benito's case file came along.

And the women who had come afterward… Benito shut out those memories. None of it was important now. None of them were important. What was important was this woman.

"I bet you were a good teacher. I bet the kids loved you," he said before brushing his lips against Calista's.

Calista almost cried out at the feel of his lips on hers. She'd never felt such instant attraction before. Such need.

She just wanted to press into him, to wrap her body around his and get as close to him as possible.

"I liked being a teacher, knowing if I did things right, the kids would get off to a good start. Everything down the road depends on having a strong foundation to start with. That's one of the reasons kids end up dropping out before they finish high school, because they start out shaky and eventually the building blocks just crumble." Benito chuckled and Calista's face heated up. "Sorry about that. I get a little intense on the subject of education."

He brushed a second light kiss over her lips before settling his mouth on hers and asking permission to enter with a sensuous stroke of his tongue. Calista's cunt clenched, sending another spasm through her clit and another wave of arousal soaking into her panties. She closed her eyes and yielded, letting him control the kiss, silently, unknowingly, communicating the secret desires of her heart. To be loved. To be cherished. To be taken care of and dominated.

A flame of intense arousal blistered through Benito. A need so fierce that only sheer willpower kept him from laying claim to every inch of her body with first his hands and then his lips. He wanted as he'd never wanted before, needed as he'd never thought it possible to need. Everything inside him hungered for this particular woman. And he had no intention of fighting it.

Holding her tightly against him, Benito plundered her mouth, tasting her, twining his tongue with hers, driving her need higher and answering her silent call with a message of his own, that he intended to have her, to claim her, to satisfy her.

They were both flushed and breathing hard by the time the song ended. Neither of them wanted to leave the dance floor, but the rapid beat of the next song didn't offer what they wanted, the slow, tight press of body against body. Benito brushed a quick kiss to her swollen lips and led her back to the table.

Another place. A different kind of woman and Dante would have claimed the next slow dance, letting the woman know he was thinking of fucking her too, setting the wheels in motion so there wouldn't be any surprises when it came time to leave.

Fuck. His hands were tied. He couldn't do that with Calista. Not here. Not now. Not with her being a cop's sister.

His cock jerked. His gut went tight.

This was unfamiliar territory.

Christ. What if Benito wanted to do her solo? What if Benito didn't want to share?

As if sensing what Dante was worrying about, Benito's gaze met his. Their twin-bond was so strong Dante didn't need to hear the words to know what Benito was thinking. *I want her. I want you to want her. I want us both to love her.*

Dante's heart threatened to shut down. He felt out of control, tense, like he was on a bridge and a freight train was barreling toward him, leaving him with only two choices—jump off or let it hit him.

Jumping off wasn't an option.

Calista was hyperaware of not only Benito's thigh pressing against hers but Dante's as well. Without a word being said, she could feel Dante's lust just as she could feel Benito's.

Her heart skipped erratically, a rapid dance that made her nipples so tight she wanted to take them between her fingers and squeeze, or better yet, offer them to both of the Giancotti brothers. Heat raced to Calista's face. She couldn't remember ever having a sexual fantasy that didn't involve sharing herself with two men. And two like these…

Her gaze met Lyric's and she could practically hear her sister-in-law shout, *Go for it!* in the second before a mischievous look settled on Lyric's face and her attention shifted to somewhere behind Calista. "Get ready, here comes Big Brother."

Reality or imagination, as soon as Lyric's words were out, Calista felt a laser blast of male aggravation and overprotectiveness boring into the back of her head. She could practically hear Kieran's voice. *Get the hell away from those two guys, Calista!*

Lyric rose from her chair, halting by Calista just long enough to lean down and whisper, "Yummy. I had to down my beer so I could cool off after watching that kiss. This is your night. Go for the gusto! Don't worry about Big Brother, I'll take care of him." Then with a laugh, she moved across the room, intercepting her husband and twining her arms around his neck, biting down on his bottom lip. "Play nice or I'm going to be mad at you," she teased, loving the way he was already hot and hard, probably already thinking about how long it would be before they could go home and fuck.

Kieran's arms went around Lyric, automatically tightening so she was flush against his body. "Baby, I better not find out you had anything to do with them being here," he growled before covering her lips with his and thrusting his tongue into her mouth aggressively.

The little hellion did what she always did, rubbed against him like a cat in heat, tormenting him with thoughts of her bare, wet cunt. Son of a bitch. He was crazy about his wife. It'd embarrass the hell out of him if she didn't make him feel so good.

Lyric laughed and pulled away. "I'm innocent this time," she said and let him lead her back to the table.

"Tough break about the Mitchell kid," Kieran said to Dante after being introduced to Benito.

Dante shrugged. "In the wrong place at the wrong time. Damned uniformed patrol should have caught it."

Kieran grunted in acknowledgment. "They got you on a desk?"

"No. Administrative leave, I don't go in unless I'm called."

"What about the other kids?"

"Both of them lawyered up with James Morrisey."

Kieran grimaced and turned his attention to his sister. "How many hands of poker did it take for Bulldog to give you the job?"

She flushed. "Maybe ten or fifteen." Her chin went up. "Not just a job, but my first case."

Kieran scowled. "Bulldog already gave you a case?" Disbelief warred with protectiveness in his voice.

Calista imitated her new client and stiffened her spine until it was perfectly vertical. Oh, she knew how Kieran felt, how all the men in her family felt. Anything even remotely involving danger came squarely under the heading of *for men only*. "Yes, he did," she shot back. "Though he told me I could pull in anyone I wanted to if I needed help." Well, he hadn't said those exact words, but he'd implied them. And she knew Bulldog was very flexible — as long as the client's interests were served.

Tyler's smooth voice eased some of the tension. "So what's the case?"

Calista shot a hesitant glance at Dante, not sure she should mention the case in front of him since he was part of the San Francisco Police Department.

"Come on, doll, don't hold out on us," Tyler begged, drawing her attention back to his oh-so-gorgeous face. She couldn't help but smile. So far, he was the only person she could consistently beat at poker.

There was a subtle movement on either side of her and a jolt of fire shot through her cunt as Benito and Dante pressed their thighs more tightly against hers. Her nipples ached as the heat from Benito and Dante burned through her blood and pulled her attention away from Tyler.

Benito's fingers brushed her hair back from her face. "Don't worry about Dante, he's on leave from the department right now and I'm trying to get him to quit altogether and be more than a silent partner at Giancotti Security."

Calista looked to Lyric for a sign. Her sister-in-law shrugged. "Give us an overview."

She did, leaving out names and places, watching as her brother's scowl deepened while Tyler seemed to grow more intrigued. "Doesn't sound like the usual Crime Tells case, but count me in if you need help," Tyler said.

A muscle ticced in Kieran's cheek. "I don't like it, Calista. You've got a dead girl probably using an alias, a missing baby and big money. You follow the money and you're going to find trouble. Lots of it when you're talking that kind of money. Tell Bulldog you want Cole or Tyler to help on the case. I don't want you working this one alone. You're not ready for it."

Calista almost smiled. God, she loved her brother, even when he was being an overprotective butthead. The truth of the matter was that he didn't want her out of the kindergarten—none of the men in her family did.

Yeah, they were macho cavemen. But their hearts were in the right place. She'd decided long ago not to let them make her crazy or inadvertently crush her self-confidence as they stumbled around trying to protect her from all the dangers inherent in living—a lot of them magnified way out of proportion in their minds as a result of being cops and firemen.

The best defense was a good offense. How many times had she heard that saying during football season?

Smiling inwardly and taking a leaf from Lyric's book, Calista gave Kieran her full attention and said, "Maybe you're right. I think I heard Bulldog say Shane and Braden are finishing up the case they're working on. I'll ask him if one of them can go around with me, maybe show me the ropes, break me in and all that."

Kieran's expression went dark at the mention of Lyric's wild cousins, a Pavlovian response Calista knew he couldn't help. Next to her, Dante and Benito tensed, making her think of large jungle cats readying themselves to fight. Her heart rabbited around in her chest in response as heat curled in her belly.

Benito's hand moved to her arm, gripping her and pulling her to her feet as a slow song began playing. She went willingly, unable to stop herself from shivering when he pulled her against his body.

Kieran waited only a heartbeat before scowling at Dante and growling, "Stay away from my sister."

Dante's lips twisted into a mocking smile. "On that note, I think I'll hit the head." He rose from his chair and maneuvered toward the restroom, skirting the dance floor and getting a good look at Benito's face in the process. Christ, his brother was already halfway to thinking he was in love with Calista.

Yeah. I'd like to stay the hell away from your sister, Kieran. But it's not going to happen. Not until Benito comes to his senses. Dante's cock jerked. *Not until I get over the urge to fuck her. It's too late to get off the train tracks now.*

"Nice work, Kieran," Tyler drawled. "I'd say you qualify for the Big Brother from Hell award."

Lyric's snicker brought her husband's attention back to her. He scowled. "Baby, I'm only going to say this once. Don't encourage Calista to go out with them."

Her eyebrows went up and down. "Them? So far she's danced with Benito twice. Hardly a reason for you to get your—"

"Don't say it, baby. Don't accuse me of having my dick in a twist."

She leaned over and bit his bottom lip. "You said it, not me. And I hope you don't get your dick in a twist, because I have plans for it later on."

Tyler choked back a laugh. One of these days Kieran was going to realize he was fighting a losing battle. He didn't stand a chance in hell of curbing Lyric's "bad" influence on anyone around her. And the truth of the matter was, if he ever did manage it, life would be boring for all of them.

Kieran scowled, feeling like there was more blood in his cock than in his brain. "I mean it, Lyric. Dante's got a reputation for playing rough and sharing his women."

She had the nerve to shrug and say, "So what? People used to say the same about you." Oh yeah, she was well aware of Kieran's bad-boy reputation before they met. He and his partner Cash had swapped any number of the badge bunnies who liked to hang out at cop bars. And as far as rough play went...it was her husband's specialty and he was damn good at it.

He gritted his teeth. "I may not have cared who a woman fucked the night before or the night after I did her, but nobody fucked her while she was with me."

Lyric's gaze traveled between Benito and Dante for several long moments before returning to meet Kieran's. "*They* share, or he shares with other cops?"

The speculative look. The hot curiosity in her eyes sent more of Kieran's blood crowding into his cock. "They share."

Lyric's smile was provocative. "Hmmm. Lucky women."

Son of a bitch! That did it!

Kieran hauled her up against his body, unable to stop himself from reacting even though he knew the little hellion was playing him. "Let's go, baby. Let's see how *you* like having something shoved up your ass while I fuck you senseless."

She laughed and winked at Tyler before allowing her husband to hustle her out of the bar. *Oh yeah, bring it on.*

Amusement filled Dante as he watched Kieran and Lyric leave. So much for big brother sticking around to guard his little sister.

His attention shifted back to Benito and Calista, and his cock pulsed, pressing hard and uncomfortably against the front of his pants. Just as well. He didn't know how much longer he could take this, being on the outside and watching.

Tyler stood as Dante joined him at the table. "You heading out?" Dante asked.

"Yeah." Tyler grimaced. "Somehow I let Cole talk me into a poker game tonight. I might as well drop my money off at the door and leave."

Dante laughed. "Remind me to invite you the next time Benito and I have people over for a night of Texas Hold'em."

As they moved away from the table, Benito and Calista joined them, not stopping until they were all standing next to Tyler's car, saying goodbye to him and watching as his car disappeared at the corner.

Anticipation and desire sizzled in the air and Calista almost whimpered when Benito pulled her into his arms. His kiss was a soft whisper across her lips. "Come home with us."

Calista's heart stilled for a beat, then danced in her chest. "With both of you?"

Her stomach tightened as she waited for his answer. Something flickered in Benito's eyes. Regret? Acceptance? He smoothed his hand over her cheek. "Or just me, if that's what you want."

Her heart thundered in her ears. A new job. Her first case. And now this. Part of her almost couldn't believe it was happening.

She licked her lips, feeling nervous and yet knowing she couldn't say no. Her panties were already wet, her need a steady ache between her thighs. She'd wanted Benito from the moment she'd seen him, wanted them both, and now he was offering her a chance to live her fantasy.

She nodded and he cupped her face, once again brushing his lips softly over hers. "Both of us? Or just me?"

"Both of you," she whispered.

He deepened the kiss, mating his tongue with hers as he held her body against his, letting her know the strength of his desire.

She could feel the heat of Dante's body behind her even though they weren't touching. She could feel his heated gaze moving over her, watching as his brother took her mouth by storm.

"Let's go," Dante growled when she and Benito came up for air.

Calista smoothed her skirt in an unconscious, nervous gesture. "That's my car over there, the black Beetle. I'll follow you to your house."

Benito stroked her cheek. "We've both got cars here too. I'll lead, Dante will stay behind you."

She nodded, his words making her think of what was about to happen — of being pressed between their bodies — one in front, one behind, as she followed where they led.

Chapter Four

Benito felt as nervous as a virgin with his first woman as he guided Calista into his home. He wanted this night to be perfect for her. He wanted this night to be a turning point for all of them.

She was the one. His heart and body had agreed instantly.

He led her to the TV room, not wanting to frighten her by hurrying her to the bedroom, not wanting to risk that she'd panic and change her mind. Behind them, Dante slowed only long enough to deal with the security system, and then followed.

Benito's gut tightened when he read Dante's body language and saw the aggressive need to dominate, to be in control, radiating off his brother. Christ, he should have known this situation would trigger that response in Dante. Fuck. Being in control was how Dante had always coped. And now it was so ingrained, so much a part of his brother that Benito knew there was no changing it, even though he would have preferred Calista not see this side of Dante on their first night together.

But there was no turning back now, nothing he could do other than let Dante find out for himself that Calista was right for them, though the knowledge would only make Dante fight harder against committing himself to her. Whether Dante would admit it or not, feeling driven to dominate now, while they were sharing a woman, was a sure sign he was worried about Calista, about how important she might be to them.

Benito pulled Calista's back to his front, pausing only long enough to brush her hair out of the way before burying his face in her neck, pressing kisses along the delicate column of skin as his hands tugged her shirt out of her skirt, then slid underneath to cover her smooth, taut stomach.

Dante stopped in front of Calista, his eyes dark and hard, his face all harsh lines. His nostrils flared as his eyes moved to where Benito's hands were stroking her flat belly and dancing over her rib cage. "Take off your shirt," he ordered and heat flashed through Calista's body at the command in his voice.

She shivered, nervousness making her hesitate before obeying. Dante's eyes narrowed, his jaw tightened, and she felt the sharp whip of erotic fear. Her breath moved in and out in shallow pants. Her fingers shook as they freed the tiny buttons.

When she was done, Benito's hands moved up her body, sweeping the shirt off her shoulders before trailing down her spine and unclasping her bra. Her stomach quivered and an unexplored part of her silently begged for Dante's praise.

She'd never felt so vulnerable. So out of control. So submissive.

Dante lowered his head and covered her lips with his, his tongue thrusting in and out of her mouth in fierce domination. She whimpered, weak with need, desperate for him to pet her, to cup her breast and push his hand between her legs, to show her that he wanted her too.

When he pulled away, she would have followed if Benito hadn't been holding her in place. "Please," she whispered and felt Benito's soothing kisses along the top of her shoulder as he slid the bra off.

Dante's face flushed with lust as his eyes roamed over her bared breasts. "Beautiful," he said and she arched in reaction, begging him silently to take her tight, hard nipples between his fingers, between his lips.

He smiled with feral, masculine satisfaction and approval. His eyes never leaving her chest as Benito's hands covered her breasts, cupping and squeezing, plucking at her dark nipples and making her chest flush with arousal.

"Now the skirt," Dante said, his voice a sharp spank across her clit.

Calista shivered. Anxious, worried that he wouldn't like what he would see. That he'd be turned off by her newly bare cunt. She hadn't been with a man since Lyric's tales had helped her find the courage to explore her own sensuality and have her pubic hair removed.

Her hesitation drove the tension in the room up. Benito's hands gentled on her breasts. His kisses along her shoulder grew softer. "Take it off, Lista," he whispered, "don't make him punish you. Not tonight. Not this first time together."

She was shaking all over, fine tremors that fired along her nerve endings and burned her soul. The zipper gave and her skirt dropped to the floor, leaving her standing in heels and midnight-black panties.

"Good girl," Benito whispered, one hand sliding down her flat belly, the feel of his rough palm against her smooth, quivering abdomen making her feel delicately feminine.

When he got to the waistband of her panties, her stomach tightened and Benito pressed a kiss to her shoulder as his fingers slipped underneath the fabric and found her clit. She cried out, bucking into his hand as pleasure shot through her.

"You like that, don't you, sweetheart?" he whispered. "You're so wet, so hot and slick. Dante's going to go crazy when he sees you."

Benito's mouth settled at the spot where her neck met her shoulder, his kisses changing from gentle comfort to sucking bites as his fingers teased her engorged clit, circling, stroking, pressing, determining how she liked to be touched.

Calista couldn't look away, couldn't take her eyes off the sight of his fingers playing in her underwear. His touches grew more devastating, more insistent, making her whimper and sob, finally driving her to the point that her hands moved to her panties, clutching at his as she hovered on the edge of a desperate climax.

"Are you ready to take these off?" Benito whispered. "Are you ready to show Dante your beautiful little pussy?"

Her voice was barely audible as she answered, "Yes."

"Good girl," Benito said, pressing two fingers into her spasming channel, stroking in and out, rewarding her with his attention.

Her hands moved to her hips, pushing the black panties down, exposing the smooth skin of her bare cunt, exposing Benito's hand as it slid through her swollen folds.

Dante crowded closer, forcing her attention back to his face. She wet her lips nervously and his eyes narrowed. "Put your arms around my neck," he ordered.

As soon as she complied, he pulled her naked body tightly against his clothed one. Benito's hand remained trapped between her thighs, stroking and petting her until Dante's mouth descended and covered hers. She whimpered at the loss of Benito's touch, pulling back instinctively in an effort to follow him.

Dante's grip tightened in primitive reaction, his kiss becoming more dominant, more demanding. She softened, melting into him, her body trying to appease him with a show of submission.

His touch gentled and when he lifted his mouth from hers, Calista could see the satisfaction in his eyes.

Benito pushed the coffee table out of the way and then moved to the couch, pulling the dark blue futon from its frame in order to make a bed on the floor. Calista shivered, more than ready to feel them inside her.

Dante's hands dropped from her back. "Get on the bed, now."

She obeyed immediately, pausing only long enough to remove her high heels before positioning herself in the middle and watching as they undressed. Her heart raced at a dizzying pace while her lungs struggled to get enough air.

When they dropped to their knees on either side of her, she was torn between lying down and spreading her legs or giving in to her need to touch them, to kiss and explore their bodies.

Her eyes moved from one masculine face to the other, looking for a hint as to what they expected and not finding one. "Tell me what you want me to do," she finally whispered.

Benito's face lit up in a smile. He moved forward, using his body to force her backward until she was stretched out on the futon with his chest half covering hers, his cock hard and wet against her thigh. "You're so beautiful…" He pressed a kiss to her lips. "…so obedient."

The praise stroked her feminine core, satisfying her in a way that was primitive and raw. Her gaze flew to Dante, unconsciously seeking his approval too.

He lay down next to her, positioning himself in the same way Benito had, with his cock hard and heavy against her thigh. His hand moved to her cunt, his fingers sliding through her wet slit. "I didn't tell you to take off the shoes," he said, "but I'm not going to punish you for doing it. Not this time." His fingers zeroed in on her erect clit, grasping it firmly between them and applying just enough pressure that her legs widened and she pressed hard against his hand as moisture gushed from her channel and coated her swollen cunt lips and inner thighs.

Dante's smile was dark and dangerous as he released her clit and stroked her heated pussy, smearing her own juices over her so that her cunt glistened. "This is why I'm not going to punish you. Because this was a surprise and because I like this so much. I like knowing you're smooth and soft and wet down here."

He leaned in closer, so his face hovered directly over hers. "But don't think just because of this beautiful little pussy I'm going to let you get away with disobeying me in the future." His words were warm across her lips, but the sensation that burst across her cunt as his hand delivered a sharp, light slap was pure fire. "That's just a warning,

Lista, so you'll know I'm serious. You don't want to disobey me."

She whimpered and pressed her mouth to his, her lips rubbing against his in soft supplication.

"Good girl," he whispered before demanding entry with his tongue and rewarding her with a hungry, possessive kiss.

When the kiss ended, Dante leaned back, and Calista's attention shifted to Benito. Warmth curled in her belly and blossomed through her chest at the look of approval on his face. He leaned in and kissed her, his touch so tender and loving, she wanted to press herself tightly against him and wallow in his caring.

She felt breathless when the kiss ended, so needy to feel him inside of her that tears were running down her cheeks. Benito lapped them up with his tongue, soothing her with his gentle caress. "Shhh, sweetheart, it's okay. We'll give you what you need."

His lips moved from hers, trailing kisses down her neck and over the slopes of her breasts, suddenly ravenous to take her nipple in his mouth and suckle. Christ, he wanted to eat her whole, to kiss and lick and bite every inch of her, to hear her cries night after night as they both pleasured her. She was so responsive, so obedient, so open…god, so different than all the other women they'd had. He wanted to lose himself in her.

Benito's cock surged against the smooth skin of her thigh, growing wetter as more pre-cum escaped. He latched onto a dark nipple and started suckling, aware that Dante had latched on to its twin.

Calista's fingers speared through their hair, holding them both to her as she thrashed underneath them, crying and whimpering and begging, pressing upward against their thighs in a plea for them to fill her. His hand moved to pet her cunt only to find Dante's already there, stroking her smooth skin.

Benito's buttocks tightened at the thought of rubbing his cock over her bare pussy, of burying his face between her legs. At the thought of demanding that she never wear panties or bras when she was at home with him. That was his fantasy, one of his needs, and Calista had expanded it to include a bare, smooth cunt. He wanted to know she was his, that he could lift up her clothing and find succor in her body anytime he wanted it.

With a groan he left her nipple, biting and kissing downward, nudging Dante's hand aside before he latched onto Calista's delicate clit. She jerked in response, a violent movement that almost dislodged him, and at her other side Dante grunted, adjusting his position, moving up and holding her down, kissing her as Benito licked and laved and suckled, and finally tunneled into her spasming channel with his tongue until she sobbed in release. And even then, her cries still being muffled by Dante's lips, it was all Benito could do to pull back. He wanted to keep loving her, to keep pleasuring her with his mouth even if it meant coming on the sheets. But he forced his mouth away from her intoxicating mound, the urge to devour giving way to the need to share.

Christ, Dante wasn't sure how much more he could take. Between Calista's cries and the hungry sounds of Benito eating her beautiful little cunt, his cock was screaming for relief.

Benito's eyes lifted and met Dante's. Along the twin-bond, Dante conveyed his need to fuck and felt his brother's desire to have her first, along with his willingness to yield if Dante couldn't wait. Dante's gut tightened, knowing either way they were in too deep, that things would never be the same again.

They'd shared hundreds of nameless women before, but never like this. It had never gone down like this.

Christ. Whether he fucked her first or his brother did, it wouldn't be the end of it.

His hand found his own cock, taking it in a firm, rough grip as he nodded slightly, watching as Benito's face flushed with pleasure as he moved up alongside Calista and leaned down, pressing kisses over her lips, her face, whispering, "Spread your legs wider, Lista, let me love you now."

Dante eased over to allow them room, his attention absorbed by the sight of the pink, wet, feminine flesh that glistened between her swollen folds as she opened her legs wider for Benito. His penis jumped in his hand, its head already slippery. Need roared through him. The need to bury his mouth between her legs and shove his tongue into her channel like Benito had done. The need to shove his cock into her and feel her submit.

Benito moved over her and Dante's heartbeat jumped in his chest at the realization his brother intended to fuck her without a condom. She whimpered, her arms and legs wrapping around Benito, and it took every bit of Dante's control to stave off his own orgasm as Benito plunged into her, eating her cries and soft submissive sounds as he rutted on her until the two of them were writhing desperately, then clutching each other in climax.

For a long moment afterward, Benito stayed on top of Calista, weighing her down with his body as though he was struggling to pull himself out of her depths. Then finally with a groan, he rolled to the side.

Between one breath and the next, Dante was on her, in her, crazed by the feel of her hot, wet channel gripping and tightening on his penis. Christ, this was insane. But he couldn't stop himself. It was the first time in his life he'd ever been in a woman unprotected. The sight of Benito going like that had been his undoing.

His breaths were coming in pants, the pleasure so extreme he knew he was out of control, wildly racing toward the finish line. He took her wrists in his hands and held them above her head, reveling in the way she let him dominate her, in the way she was thrashing and whimpering underneath him, taking everything he gave her.

White fire raced down his spine, a hot warning that had him pistoning faster, slamming against her harder until she arched underneath, crying out as her tight channel fisted around him and jerked the seed from his body in a stream of hot agony.

Afterward he wanted to settle his body on hers, to pin her down and leave his cock crammed into the bliss of her welcoming sheath. It felt better than anything he'd ever felt in his life. It felt like coming home.

And that scared him into pulling out, to rolling away from her and trying to put some distance between them. But as soon as he did, Benito was back on her, kissing her, murmuring to her as his penis stroked in and out, loving her—making Dante's gut tighten. Christ, he didn't want this. Because in the end, it would eventually drive a rift between Benito and him.

Chapter Five

Calista woke to the feel of a masculine chest against her back and a hand smoothing over her belly and teasing between her thighs, rubbing her already erect clit and slipping into her wet channel. Without opening her eyes, she knew it was Benito. She smiled, shifting so he could touch more of her.

He pressed a kiss to her shoulder. "Okay?"

"Better than okay."

His fingers followed the flow of her arousal, tracing the moisture on her labia, her inner thighs, the crevice between her buttocks. When he found her small, puckered anus, she tensed and tried to shift away from the touch.

Benito's fingers stilled for an instant before they continued to circle and brush across her back entrance. He pressed another kiss to her shoulder and whispered, "You need to get used to this, Lista. You need to get used to having a man this way. Dante and I are both going to want to fuck you here. And then we're going to want to fuck you at the same time. One of us in your sweet little pussy and the other in your tight little ass." His palm settled over her clit, pressing and rubbing, stimulating her as his fingertips played in the crevice of her ass.

Despite the fact they'd taken her repeatedly in the living room, and they'd both reached for her in the darkness after they'd moved to the bed, Calista suddenly felt desperate, anxious, needy. Her hand settled onto

Benito's and she pressed backward, rubbing herself against his cock. "Please, Benito."

He laughed softly, his warm breath flowing across her heart. "If you want me, then take me."

She almost cried out when he rolled away from her, but his hands reached for her, urging her to straddle him. She went willingly, her heart lurching at the look in his face, at his sheer, overwhelming beauty as he lay with his long black hair spread out on the pillows around him.

She couldn't resist the temptation of his diamond-studded earring. Bending over, she trapped his fully aroused penis between their bodies as her tongue traced his ear, exploring it intimately before moving to his earlobe. His hands gripped her hips, trying to lift her so he could slide his cock into her, but Calista resisted, extending the sensual torture by moving to his tight male nipples.

"Lista," he said, the hint of pleading in his voice filling her with feminine power.

She moved to his other nipple, laving and biting and sucking until they were both shivering and panting. Until he took control, forcing her onto his cock.

Calista cried out at the feel of his hard, thick penis inside her. His hands tightened on her hips and he groaned, helping her find a rhythm that had them surging against each other, pleasing each other until they both went tight with orgasm.

Afterward he pulled her down so she lay on his chest. "I'd like to wake up like this every morning," he said, smoothing his hand along her spine.

She tensed, instinctively trying to protect herself from reading too much into his words as reality slowly intruded and some of her confidence faded. What now? Shower? Dress in last night's clothes? She grimaced at the thought. Awkwardly exchange phone numbers? Run home?

Calista could feel a blush rising to her face. She didn't know how to get out of the house without making it obvious she was clueless about how to handle "the morning after living the ultimate fantasy". She'd had exactly three sexual partners, and she'd known all of them months before even dating them, let alone going to bed with them.

She shivered, wondering if Dante was still here, then decided it didn't matter. She wasn't sorry it had happened. A little embarrassed about not knowing how to handle this part of it, but she wasn't sorry.

Gathering her courage, she said, "I'd better get going, I've got a case to start working on."

Benito's arms tightened, hugging her to him. His chin rubbed against the top of her head.

This was a first. He didn't want her to leave at all, much less leave without promising to come back at the end of the day, to eat dinner with him and sleep in his bed. But he didn't have a clue what to say to get her to agree.

Her body tensed slightly and he knew she was going to pull away. His arms tightened automatically. "I think Dante was going to go grab some fresh bagels. Eat breakfast with us before you leave."

"Okay." There was the slightest hesitation and Benito thought her cheek felt warmer against his chest. "I need to get my clothes."

Her voice betrayed her awkwardness, and protectiveness surged through him, flooding his heart with warmth and making his penis pulse against her abdomen. When she laughed softly, rubbing the smooth skin of her belly against his cock like a satisfied kitten, he couldn't help but smile. He hugged her again and pressed a kiss against her silky hair. This was paradise and he didn't want to leave. Christ, he'd die if he couldn't get back here.

A sharp stab of fear spiked through his heart at the thought. "Come over for dinner tonight." When she didn't answer immediately, the fear grew and curled in his gut.

"I don't know if I can, Benito. This case is really important to me. I need to go to San Francisco. I may still be there at dinnertime."

"Let Dante go with you. Let him help. He knows the city."

"And the city knows him too right now. His face and name have been all over the papers."

An unfamiliar panic gripped Benito and he could feel his heart racing against her chest. "You don't want to be seen with him."

Calista pulled away so she was leaning on her elbows, her face above his, her hair falling like a silky black curtain around them. "I doubt your brother wants to spend his time off trailing around after me and having people stare at him, maybe even sling insults and curses at him."

Benito's hands slid down her sides, briefly cupping her hips before settling at the base of her spine and pressing her lower body tightly to his so that her sweet, bare cunt burned against his cock.

Christ. He was already addicted to the feel of her skin against his, to her softness and gentle spirit.

"Let me ask him if he'll go with you," Benito said, lifting his face and brushing his lips against hers in a pleading kiss. "Bulldog has a reputation for being flexible, as long as it serves his clients. With Dante's knowledge and connections, you could wrap this up faster." His tongue washed across the seam of her lips, coaxing her to open for him. When she did, he deepened the kiss, intent on persuading her to spend time with his brother, to come back here at the end of the day so they could all three be together again.

"Okay," she sighed in surrender, her acceptance going straight to his cock. Without taking his lips from hers, he rolled her underneath him and pressed his penis home—into the warm, tight heaven of her channel.

With gentle, slow strokes, followed by deep, soul-touching plunges, he brought them both to orgasm. And even when they were both sated, Benito hated to pull out. The pleasure of being inside Calista, of feeling her hot sheath tighten like a wet fist around his unprotected cock, was overwhelming, intense—a first for him—and he was suddenly glad he'd never experienced any other woman like this. She was a gift to him, to Dante, and he liked knowing that even though he and his brother had fucked a lot of women, they'd never gone in unprotected, never given as much of themselves—until Calista.

Dante moved around the house restlessly. His cock screamed for him to go back to bed, to fuck Calista again before she left.

With the bedroom door open, her cries had just about made him go in and join them. His hand moved to cover the straining bulge of his penis.

Christ. What he really wanted to do was take her at the same time as Benito did, but unlike some of the women they'd brought home with them, she was too innocent, too inexperienced to do it without preparing her first.

White-hot need pulsed through his penis at the thought of being the one to train her for that kind of pleasure. The images almost drove him to his knees.

Shit. He needed to get her out of here so things could go back to normal.

Like that was going to happen. He and Benito were already sliding toward a shitload of pain. Only Benito wouldn't see it.

Dante's gut tightened when she walked in, hair in a ponytail and damp from a shower, wearing one of Benito's light blue shirts. The arms were rolled up, the shirttail tied around her slim waist. Christ. The symbolism wasn't lost on him. Benito wanted to keep her.

She smiled hesitantly when she saw him and a blush washed over her face. "Morning," she murmured, her eyes skittering away. "Benito said you got some bagels."

Dante gritted his teeth, fighting the urge to pull her into his arms and kiss her. "Yeah, they're on the table. You want some cream cheese?"

"Sure."

"What about coffee?"

"For a cup of coffee, you'll be my hero."

He moved over to the counter, feeling her eyes on him, but when he looked up from pouring her drink, her gaze was elsewhere though the faint flush of color remained on her cheeks. His heart clenched and his cock jerked, both of them wanting him to move over and pull her into his arms, to reestablish the connection.

Benito walked in, his gaze shifting between Dante and Calista before he moved to where she stood, his hands going to her hips as he guided her back to his chest. He nuzzled a kiss against her neck, his eyes holding Dante's and conveying an unmistakable message, an unmistakable challenge. *You can decide to walk away from her if you want to, but I'm not.*

Fuck. Dante set the cup of coffee down on the counter separating them and moved around so that he stood in front of Calista, crowding into her personal space, the sheer force of his presence making her tilt her face upward and focus on him.

The flush deepened, but he knew from the way her body tensed in anticipation and her lips parted slightly that it wasn't embarrassment this time. His cock pulsed, hungry for her. He pressed in, cupping her face and holding her steady as his lips covered hers and his tongue plunged into her mouth, tangling with her tongue, mating with it in the wet, heated darkness. Reclaiming the right to touch her at will.

Between their bodies, he felt Benito's hands cover her breasts, squeezing and tugging at her nipples, his added attention making her whimper and rub herself against the front of Dante's jeans.

Dante groaned. Much more of this and he wasn't going to be able to stop himself from bending her over the counter and fucking her.

Christ, they were already in too deep with her. Her presence was already driving a wedge between Benito and him. Forcing him to make choices he didn't want to make, to take risks with his heart he'd sworn never to take.

And now this, one kiss, and he was so hard all he wanted to do was get his cock back into her, to feel her tight little channel squeeze around him and bathe him in a hot wash of desire and liquid arousal. Goddamn if he was going to let Calista take his control. To pussy-whip him like she was on her way to doing to his brother.

Yeah, he'd take what she had to offer, but on his terms. He'd play with her until Benito came to his senses and they could go back to uncomplicated sex.

I like them easy and I like to share them with you. End of story, Benito.

Dante pulled away and stepped back, trying to get his breathing under control and slow the wild, erratic beat of his heart. To keep her effect on him hidden behind hard eyes and a face that didn't show any emotion.

With a flick of his wrist, he looked at his watch and back at his brother. "I thought you had an important meeting this morning."

Benito pressed another kiss to Calista's neck before releasing her and picking up the mug of coffee, taking a sip before passing it off to her. "Yeah, I do. I need to get a move on or I'll be late."

Benito's hand brushed Calista's hip and Dante gritted his teeth. Christ, his brother couldn't seem to keep his hands off her.

"You need cream or sugar for your coffee, sweetheart? Dante forgets other people don't necessarily take it black."

"Both," she answered, looking everywhere except at Dante and causing his cock to surge with satisfaction.

Fuck. Her nervousness around him just turned up the heat, calling up his darker desires for a completely submissive woman.

Benito handed the half-and-half and sugar off to Calista then reached for a bagel, his voice casual when he asked, "What about you, Dante? You have any plans for the day?"

Dante shrugged. "Haven't gotten that far yet."

"Calista has to spend the day in the city, working on her case." Benito paused long enough to take another sip of coffee from her mug. "If she gets done early enough, we could have dinner together."

Even though Dante had known it was coming, his gut tightened. He couldn't have her here again tonight and not fuck her. Hell, it was taking every bit of his control to keep his distance now, and he already knew the more he was with her, the more he was going to want her—and the more he was going to need her soft and submissive and yielding underneath him. Dante gritted his teeth and remained silent, knowing from Benito's expression that his brother was well aware of what he was thinking.

Benito took another sip of coffee. "I thought maybe if you're not doing anything, you'd be interested in going with Calista to the city. You know your way around, it could speed things up so she could get back early enough to spend time with us."

When Dante didn't answer right way, Calista's fingers smoothed over her skirt in the anxious gesture he'd noticed before. Her eyes met Benito's and something passed between them that had Dante's gut tightening at being left out. "I'd better hit the road," she said. "I can call you later and tell you how it's going."

"I'll walk you out to your car," Benito said. "Take a bagel with you."

"You going to your place first?" Dante growled, mad at Benito for falling so hard, so fast, mad at her for being such a temptation, and mad at himself for going along with something he knew was going to end in a shitload of pain and a world of hurt.

"Yes," she answered, reaching for a bagel.

"I'll follow you there, then we can take my car to the city."

Chapter Six

Calista pulled the Bug into her driveway and stopped, casting a quick glance in her rearview mirror. Dante was right behind her in his Wrangler.

Not that she'd tried to lose him on the way, but now that she was home... She bit her bottom lip and momentarily rested her head on the steering wheel, wishing she was alone so she could get her bearings and put things in perspective.

In one day her world had completely rearranged itself—from the interview with Bulldog, to getting her first case, to the Giancotti brothers...to sleeping with both Dante and Benito.

She didn't regret it. She was honest enough with herself to admit she wanted to keep doing it. But right at this moment, she wished she hadn't given in to Benito and agreed to let him ask Dante to go with her to San Francisco.

Benito she could handle. All she had to do was think about him and she felt warm from the inside out. She'd never felt so feminine, so cared for, so well...loved. Her womb fluttered and her heart gave a little jolt though her mind shied away from making what had happened more than what it was.

She looked up and watched Dante get out of his car, dark shades and an attitude that sent a primal rush of fear through her. He was more than she could handle.

She shivered, remembering what she'd thought when she first saw him last night. Only now it wasn't speculation, now she knew firsthand. He *was* a walking orgasm, a sexual animal that could give a woman a night she'd never forget.

But the only thing he was offering was his body, and only while it suited him. Which was fine if a woman could handle it.

The trouble was, Calista knew she couldn't.

It didn't take a degree in psychology—which she had along with her degree in early childhood education—to understand why she'd responded to his dominating commands last night, why she craved them, why the combination of Benito and Dante was lethal to her.

Between the two of them, they could make her feel completely loved, completely safe, completely uninhibited. It was a heady, addictive mix.

And an illusion.

She needed to keep that in mind, otherwise she was going to end up really, really hurt. She couldn't share herself with someone and keep her feelings locked up. She couldn't separate her body from her heart and mind.

Sighing, she climbed out of the car and looked down the street, not surprised to see Tyler's car still in his driveway. He was not an early morning person.

Dante came to a halt next to her. She flipped through her keys and found the one to the house. "You can go in if you want. I need to get my dogs from Tyler."

His eyebrows lifted slightly but he made no move to reach for the keys. "I'll wait here."

Calista bit down on her bottom lip. Well, good thing Tyler already knew where she'd been, though she had a feeling he was going to be surprised at seeing Dante with her this morning and not Benito. She would have laughed if her emotions weren't edging into total chaos.

She sighed and made her way down the sidewalk, passing Cady's house, still full of Cady's stuff until Bulldog decided who was going to live in it once Cady completely moved out. Erin's house was next, though Erin was still out of town, working a case with Dasan Nahtailsh, a bounty hunter who looked like he'd stepped off the cover of a historical romance novel entitled *Savage Surrender*, Calista snickered, or *Savage Fantasy*. There was already a betting pool going as to whether or not Erin was going to end up married to him.

She turned at the next house, Tyler's house—also owned by Bulldog, and one of the perks for working at Crime Tells. Free housing as long as the house was kept in good repair. In the San Francisco Bay area, it was like striking gold.

She knocked on Tyler's door and set off a chorus of barking. That'd wake him up if he wasn't already out of bed.

The barking grew louder as the dogs got to the front door. Two distinctive, energetically happy voices, slowly followed by three additional voices.

A sleep-tousled, bare-chested, barefooted Tyler opened the door and stepped out on the stoop. Five dachshunds danced out at the same time. All excited, all waving their tails, though three of them moving at a slower speed.

"Sorry, I would have let myself in, but I didn't know for sure whether or not you were alone," Calista said, taking in the sheer gorgeousness of the man in front of her.

She'd always had a thing for dark-haired, dark-eyed men, but she'd have made an exception for Tyler. Even her grandmother was affected by him! She called him *that stunning buccaneer.*

Tyler rubbed his hand over his smooth chest. "Fat chance. After I finished playing poker with the Maguires and a few of their friends, I didn't have enough money left to put gas in the car so I could get to a bar, much less buy a lady a drink so she could make me feel better."

Calista laughed and crouched down, petting all the dogs. "I'd say it couldn't have been that bad, except for the fact that you're the only one *I* can usually beat."

Tyler's laugh was like warm honey. "Rub it in, doll. At least I've got the babe-magnets for times like this when my funds are low and my ego is busted. They may not be manly dogs, but they sure work with the ladies."

"Like you really need a couple of little dogs to attract women." She gathered two of the three gray-muzzled red dachshunds in her arms and stood. "Thanks for taking care of my old guys for me. I know they'd have been all right overnight without me, but…"

"No problem. Consider me your backup." He scooped up the two high-energy dogs and held one under each arm.

"Thanks again." She leaned in and gave him a kiss on the cheek. "Now I'd better get to work on my case.

"Be careful, doll. Don't get hurt."

For a minute she thought he was talking about the case. But then his gaze shifted to where Dante was leaning against the Bug. "Try not to get in too deep."

She had a feeling it was already too late for that. Shifting her attention to the old dog half-resting on her feet, she said, "Come on, guys, let's go home."

Christ. If she had any idea about the fantasies rushing through his mind right now, she wouldn't be walking toward him like she didn't have a care in the world.

Fuck. He hadn't liked seeing her cozying up to Tyler. Hadn't liked the way her body was soft and accepting, casually moving in and out of the other man's personal space. And when she'd crouched down to pet the dogs, then looked back up at Tyler's face while he'd been one small step and a pair of jeans away from being able to guide her mouth right to his cock…

Son of a bitch… While she was fucking them, she belonged to them—totally, completely, in every way—and everything about her should scream *taken*.

He hadn't wanted to feel this way…not about any woman…but there it was, and he couldn't think of a single reason why he should fight it. Benito had set this thing into motion and he was just going to have to live with the consequences.

So was she.

Dante moved away from the car and followed her into the house, giving her just enough time to put the dogs she was carrying down before grabbing her arms and pulling her against him. "I didn't like seeing you fawning all over him," he growled, his balls tightening at the little rush of feminine fear he saw in her face. And when she licked her lips, a jolt of pure fire rushed through his cock.

Every cell in Calista's body responded to his tone, to the hard, possessive expression on his face. It struck right to her core, hitting a primitive part of her that craved a dominant man.

"I wasn't fawning over him, I was just thanking him for looking after my dogs," she whispered, lowering her eyes as her body softened instinctively, cuddling into his hardness.

His body remained tense and she risked a look upward. A muscle ticced in his cheek. "It pissed me off to see you kneeling at his feet like you were begging for his cock."

Heat rushed to Calista's face. "We're just friends!"

"Keep it that way. Benito and I don't share with anyone but each other." His grip on her arms loosened though his expression was still tight. "Remember what I said last night. You don't want to disobey me, Lista. Right now the only thing keeping me from disciplining you is that we need to get to the city."

Pure need rushed through her veins at his words. A dark craving she couldn't help, but had never had a chance to explore before. Her inner thighs were wet, her clit was standing at attention. She barely recognized herself as she leaned in and rubbed her cheek against his shirt, whispering, "Please don't be mad at me. Let me show you how sorry I am."

His breath escaped on a long shudder, his hands dropping away from her arms as he widened his stance. "Show me, then."

Not taking her eyes off his face, she slowly unbuttoned his shirt, pressing kisses to his warm flesh as her mouth followed her fingers downward. When she got to his waist, she looked away so she could undo his belt and then his fly, spreading the jeans open and nuzzling her face against the rigid length of his still-covered penis.

It jerked against her cheek, spotting his Jockeys with the evidence of his leaking desire. His cock strained to rise above the waistband and she took the elastic in her teeth, pulling downward, freeing just the tip of him before washing it with her tongue, exploring its leaking slit and caressing it with her lips.

He speared his fingers through her hair, his hips thrusting slightly in demand. "Don't tease me, Lista," he warned.

Her hands slipped to his hips, tugging his jeans and underwear down far enough for his cock to spring free. She nuzzled her cheek against hot, hard, masculine flesh before leaning back and exploring his balls with the fingers of one hand while the others stroked his shaft.

He groaned in response and she thrilled at the way his buttocks were clenched, at the way the muscles on his abdomen and thighs were tight as he held himself under control.

She looked up at his face again, wanting to see the effect of what she was doing to him, wanting to see his expression as she licked and kissed along his shaft before sucking at his testicles.

His face hardened into a feral mask of pleasure. And at the sight of it, a wave of feminine satisfaction raged through her. She moved back up his cock, once again returning to the head, striking it and exploring it with her tongue until he growled, "Suck it, Lista, now."

She moaned and took him in her mouth, thrilling at the way his fingers tightened in her hair, at the way his breathing became labored as his control slipped away until finally he was crying out in pleasure, his body shaking with it as he came.

She held him in her mouth until his movements had gentled and his breathing had slowed. Only then did she pull back, raising her face once again to look at his.

Christ, he'd never experienced anything like what she'd just done to him. And now, seeing her on her knees...

Satisfaction raged through him at how submissive she was, how much she craved being dominated, how easy it was to read her need. She was shaking with it, soft and vulnerable in a way he'd only experienced in his fantasies.

He cupped her face in his hand, rubbing her cheek in silent praise before saying, "Let's go into the bedroom, baby. You need me to take care of you before we leave."

She rose to her feet and he followed, hesitating only long enough to pull his pants up. When they got to her bedroom, he pulled her to him, one arm around her waist while his free hand stroked the back of her leg, moving upward underneath her skirt. A shudder went through him at the feel of her naked ass. Christ, if he'd known she wasn't wearing panties...

He buried his face in her hair as his fingers slipped between her thighs. "Spread your legs, Lista."

She obeyed and he explored her puffy cunt lips and dripping slit as she whimpered and shivered against his chest. "It's okay, baby, I'm not going to make you go to San Francisco like this."

He eased her backward until she was close to the bed, then he released her. "Take your skirt and shoes off and lie down." When she did as he'd instructed, he said, "Now scoot up and spread your legs so I can look at that beautiful little pussy."

Her thighs quivered as she obeyed, her chest moved up and down in shallow pants. "That's a good girl," Dante said, easing down on the bed, his elbow resting next to her hip so he could take in the sight of her wet, swollen flesh.

Christ, he wanted to dive right in, to bury his face between her thighs and eat her up. It took all his control to say, "Touch yourself, Lista. Let me see you play with yourself."

Heat spread across both her face and the bare skin of her mound. Her fingers nervously toyed with the dark blue comforter. And when she didn't immediately comply, he punished her with a spank to her cunt.

She whimpered and arched upward, the color of her aroused flesh deepening as more blood rushed to her labia and clit. Tentatively her fingers moved to the sensitive area, delving into her channel until they were slick and wet before moving to her engorged knob.

Fire raced to Dante's cock at the sight of her touching herself. Christ, he was almost as lost in her as Benito was. "Make yourself come," he growled, unable to stop himself from leaning in closer, from drowning in the smell of her arousal.

She hesitated a heartbeat, then touched herself more firmly, her fingers circling and stroking the underside of her clit, making him ache to replace them with his tongue. A second hand joined the first, its fingers tunneling into her slit, then retreating in order to hold her clit steady as she rubbed across its tiny, unprotected head.

It took every bit of control he had not to suck her small organ into his mouth as she arched upward, whimpering and crying out his name until finally jerking in release and settling back on the comforter.

Dante moved then, giving in to the fantasy that had been riding him since he'd first seen her bare pussy, the fantasy that had intensified when he saw Benito eating her. He grabbed her hips and buried his face between her legs, hungrily licking and sucking at hot swollen flesh until he couldn't hold back any longer, couldn't keep himself from shoving his tongue into her tight channel and fucking her with it until she screamed and bathed him in her orgasm.

Christ. He felt as horny as a convict just leaving prison. And the scent and taste of her arousal only intensified the craving to have her in every way a man can have a woman.

Dante lifted his face from between her thighs, taking in Calista's flushed features and submissive body language. His cock jerked in response, hard again, desperate to feel her heat and wetness as he tunneled in and out of her clinging channel.

He'd denied himself earlier, when he'd wanted to bend her over the table and start the day by fucking her in the kitchen. But that was before he saw her with Tyler. "Get on your hands and knees," he ordered, standing and freeing his penis as she did what he'd told her to do, then anticipated his next command and spread her legs, presenting her wet, swollen vulva to him.

His cock pulsed as fiery lust filled it, making him tighten his grip so he wouldn't come over the creamy globes of her tanned ass, then tighten even further when the image of doing that sent shards of icy heat through his shaft. He fought off the need to come—wanting to memorize the sight of her bare cunt, its secrets unfolding for his pleasure, its lips glistening like a hungry mouth.

For several long moments he just looked, fierce pleasure rushing through him as she began shaking with need, with anticipation, with a primitive fear that he wouldn't mount her. Like an exotic flower, the petals of her sex grew, opening wider as more blood rushed to her labia. Arousal gathered on the plump folds, a nectar meant to attract, to lure.

Dante couldn't resist any longer. He joined her on the bed, taking her hips in his hands and holding her into position as his cock rammed home in a frenzied, rough mating that had them both crying out as they rushed for release.

Chapter Seven

Dante cut a look over at Calista as they drew near to San Francisco and his gut went tight. He wanted her. By himself. With his brother. Both. Either. It didn't matter.

What they'd done at her house had only ratcheted up the need.

Fuck. This was a train wreck waiting to happen and there were going to be casualties.

She wasn't like any other woman he'd spent time with. Christ, her refrigerator was covered with crayon drawings! Her walls had pictures of her with her students, and her shelves were loaded with Tinkertoys, Legos and boxes of learning games. Everything about her screamed "let's get married and have babies".

He should walk now. He knew he should.

A fist wrapped around his heart and squeezed painfully. Jesus. He knew he should, but he couldn't. He was already in too deep.

"So what's with all the dachshunds?" he asked, trying to take his mind off where this thing with her was heading. "And how is it that Tyler lives three houses down?"

She laughed and slanted him a look. "Lyric. My grandmother hired Lyric to retrieve her three dachshunds when they were stolen—which Lyric did—but she also ended up with a lot of other dachshunds. My old guys were the last ones who needed homes. I agreed to adopt them if I could find a place to live that allowed pets. And since Lyric was marrying Kieran, Bulldog said I could move into her house. Well, technically, the house belongs to Bulldog. He owns Tyler's house, the two in between ours, and three around the corner. Lyric's cousins live in those."

Son of a bitch. Wouldn't that be fun if word got back to Big Brother that both he and Benito were fucking Calista.

"What's the address?" he asked as they started seeing freeway exit signs. Calista opened the file and gave it to him. "Marina District," he said, cutting her a quick look when she didn't say anything. "Marina Green. Sailboats. Kite flying. Ring any bells?"

She bit her bottom lip and it was all he could do not to lean over and kiss her. "I think I've seen pictures of it on the news."

He couldn't keep himself from smiling. "Don't get to San Francisco much, I take it."

"Almost never. Though I guess that might change since I'm working for Crime Tells now."

A tornado of unexpected emotion swirled through Dante's heart at her casual comment. Christ, what was wrong with him? He'd never wanted any woman making claims on his personal time or staying at his apartment in the city longer than it took for a night of casual sex. And now he wanted to grab Calista and force her to admit Crime Tells' business wasn't the only thing that would bring her to San Francisco.

He parked the car and got out, somehow managing to resist the urge to pull her into his arms, to kiss and stroke her until she told him what he wanted to hear. Goddammit. She was twisting him up inside.

They moved up the walkway to the small apartment complex and Dante retreated from the chaos of his emotions by slipping into cop mode.

The place was well cared for despite being an older building. Three units on the bottom, three units on the top. Smaller than the majority of apartment complexes in the Marina District, but similar to others in this neighborhood. Freshly mowed grass, a couple of flower boxes. Probably owned by someone with money, someone who could afford to reduce the rent in order to keep a manager on site.

Calista stopped in front of apartment A and unlocked the door. Dante had to check the impulse to put her behind him and go in first.

The place was well lit, clean and tidy, tasteful, almost like something out of a newspaper spread. Bank of windows in front of them, on the other side of the living room, kitchen to the left, separated by a counter. Bedroom through a door to the right, windows letting in light from that direction too since it was an end unit. Couple of other doors, closed. Probably a bathroom and a closet.

No pictures other than typical San Francisco art shots on the walls, no shoes under the coffee table, no glasses on the counter. Dante grunted. If the bedroom was the same, this trip was going to be a bust. So far the apartment had all the ambience of a hotel room.

"It doesn't look lived in," Calista said, echoing his thoughts. "It doesn't even feel lived in."

She moved into the bedroom, going straight to the closet and opening it. He followed, stopping in the doorway and leaning against the jamb, the instinct to get involved and actively help warring with the instinct to keep his distance. He rode the fence until she shot him a look and said, "If you're just going to stand there and stare at me, maybe you could wait in the car. It's hard to concentrate with you doing that."

Amusement flashed through him. Christ, she was the complete opposite of the ball-busting women he had to work with in the police department. He pushed away from the doorframe. "I'll take the dresser."

Calista nodded and turned her attention to the clothes hanging in the closet. She wasn't much of a clothes hound, not much of a temptation to be one when she spent most of her time around sticky-fingered children and messy arts and crafts projects — not to mention the occasional toilet training failures. Still, she knew enough to see Jessica had liked stylish, name-brand clothing and shoes — and that none of them had been designed for a pregnant woman.

Calista checked pockets, the floor of the closet and the shelf at the top with the same results. There was nothing personal, nothing that revealed anything about Jessica Winston other than the fact she liked nice clothing and appeared to take care of her possessions.

"Anything?" Calista asked as she joined Dante at the dresser.

"Nothing." There was no inflection in his tone, but she'd been around cops her entire life, so she read between the lines.

"You think she was involved in something criminal."

He scowled and met her eyes. "I don't like this. Nobody lives like this unless they're on the run, getting ready to run, or they've got something to hide and they're overly paranoid about the secret getting out."

"She was getting ready to go to Hawaii. Maybe she was planning to move there."

"Maybe." Once again his tone held no inflection but she knew what he wasn't saying and agreed with it. This was more than someone getting ready to move. This was someone erasing all trace of herself.

Calista moved over to the bed and knelt down so she could look under it. She didn't expect to find anything, but she looked anyway. Dante joined her, pulling up the mattress to make sure nothing was hidden between it and the box springs. When he dropped it back in place, he said, "I'll take the living room and the kitchen, you can take the bathroom."

The bathroom held the usual assortment of feminine products, along with a used toothbrush and a skewed hand towel next to the sink. Calista stood for a few minutes, taking in everything—including the expensive cosmetics and personal items—before reaching the conclusion that Jessica had intended to come back to her apartment, but she'd been prepared to abandon it if she needed to.

Calista moved to the sink, opening the drawers and then the cabinet. A small trash can occupied the area underneath the sink, along with an assortment of cleaning supplies and way too much toilet paper crowded into such a small space. She tilted the trashcan to look inside and set off an avalanche of toilet paper rolls. With a groan she reached into the cabinet to try and restore order, moving some of the cleaning supplies and in the process dislodging a small glass drug vial.

Finally! Excitement chased through her as she retrieved the vial and read the label. Puzzlement followed. It was for a fertility drug. She recognized the name because her last teacher's aide had been trying to get pregnant and had shared the hope and disappointment-filled journey with Calista.

She pocketed the vial and restacked the toilet paper before escaping to the living room. Dante was studying the contents of the refrigerator. "About what you'd expect, given the way the rest of this place looks," he said, closing the door and turning toward Calista. "Bare essentials and frozen dinners. I don't think Jessica ate at home very often. A couple of boxes in the trash, along with some soda cans and coffee grounds."

"I think she was planning on coming back here, but she was prepared to abandon the place if she had to. Did you find any suitcases?"

Surprise flashed across his face and she wondered if he was surprised she'd come to that conclusion on her own, or surprised because she'd come up with something he hadn't. "No suitcases," he said.

Her hand went to her pocket and she rubbed the vial as though it was a worry-stone, unsure whether or not to share it with him. Her expression must have given her away. His face tightened and he moved to stand in front of her, crowding into her personal space as his fingers speared through her hair, forcing her to meet his gaze.

"Don't hold out on me, Lista. I don't like the feel of this case and I'm not going to let you work it alone."

Her heart turned over. On some level she knew she should protest and point out that this was *her* case and he wasn't involved, not any more than just as a favor to

Benito, and just for today. But the truth of the matter was that she wanted to spend time with him, to get to know him better outside of the bedroom. She wanted him to see her as something other than a…she didn't want to be just one of hundreds of women he and Benito had shared.

With Benito it was easy to believe it was more…but with Dante…

And besides, she didn't like the feel of this case either. Everyday people didn't live like this. And someone who'd taken fertility drugs to get pregnant and had delivered a baby would have tons of baby pictures around, even if they'd already moved the baby furniture out. Her brows drew together as it suddenly hit her why a twenty-three-year-old would be taking fertility drugs.

Dante's fingers tightened in her hair, drawing her attention back to him. His eyes were narrowed, his features even tighter.

She bit her bottom lip nervously and watched as his nostrils flared and his focus shifted to her mouth. He leaned in so close that their breaths mingled. "I'm trying to give you some space here, baby. I'm trying to keep what I want from you in the bedroom separate from the case, but you don't want to push too many of my buttons, Lista. You don't want to hold out on me." This time there was an edge to his voice that sent a shiver up her spine and a flood of moisture to her panties.

"Okay," she whispered against his mouth, her body going soft and submissive as he closed the distance, pulling her against him so she felt the strength of his muscles, the hardness of his cock.

His lips covered hers, his tongue was fierce and demanding as it pushed into her mouth, stroking and plunging until she whimpered with pleasure and submission. The sound satisfied him, gentled him, changed the kiss into a reward for giving him what he wanted — a reward that reached deep inside of her, bathing her heart and womb with need.

When he pulled away, she wanted to follow, to rub her lips against his, to slip her tongue along the seam of his mouth and plead with him to pet her, to love her. He smiled and ran his hand along her spine, stopping at the base and holding her tight against his erection for a long moment before releasing her and stepping back.

Calista pulled the glass vial from her pocket and handed it to him. "I recognize it. It's a fertility drug."

Dante's eyebrows went up. "How old was your client's daughter?"

"Twenty-three. Do you ever watch *Crime Scene Investigation*?"

A muscle jerked in his cheek. "The intelligent criminal's guide to not leaving behind trace evidence and getting caught? Yeah, I watch *CSI* with Benito sometimes."

"In one of their episodes, a woman had a gambling addiction and she was taking fertility drugs, then selling her eggs. I can't remember if they gave any details, but after I saw that episode, there was an article in the paper about the ethics of women selling their eggs. The article focused on how some wealthy couples have even placed ads in school newspapers to attract students into selling their eggs, and even then the students are screened for looks as well as intelligence. They gave an example of a couple who had placed an ad in a bunch of Ivy League schools offering fifty thousand dollars for the *perfect* egg. I think the woman had to be athletic, have SAT scores of fourteen hundred, and be over a certain height."

"Jesus," Dante said. "Let's talk to the apartment manager, then I want to stop by my apartment. I've got a computer there. We can dig around on the Internet."

Calista nodded, thinking about the picture of Jessica. She'd been a beautiful girl, and if she'd been selling her eggs, was it such a leap to think she might produce a child and put it up for "adoption"? Calista's stomach tightened, remembering the conversations she'd had with her aide.

The world was full of unwanted infants and children, foster care systems were loaded with abused, troubled and just hard-to-place kids. But the reality remained. Desperate couples who couldn't conceive, even with fertility treatments, still wanted a newborn baby that looked like them, and they were willing to shower birth-mothers with exorbitant gifts and expense reimbursements in order to adopt a child. Calista's heart ached just thinking about it.

She followed Dante out of the apartment, stopping long enough to lock the door behind her. Bulldog would have to be told where this might be heading.

"Which apartment is the manager in?" Dante asked.

"C."

They moved to the other end unit but no one was home. Calista fingered the Crime Tells business card in her back pocket. It was a generic card for the agency, but it would be easy enough to put her name and phone number on the back, along with a request for the manager to call her, but...she'd feel better if she could watch the manager's expression and actually talk in person. "I think I'll call from your place. Maybe we could swing by later if the manager is home."

"No problem."

They did make the rounds, leaving cards at the other four apartments before getting back into Dante's car.

"This is the Sunset District, right?" Calista asked as they neared Golden Gate Park.

Dante chuckled. "The street name give it away?"

Calista smiled, entranced by how different his face looked when he lightened up. "Maybe. So you live around here, in walking distance of the park?" She couldn't help thinking how much fun her old guys would have tooling around the park, meeting people, sniffing and snoozing in the grass.

"Yeah, we're a couple of blocks away from my apartment now." He shot her a look. "Don't expect anything fancy. It's a studio. I keep it because I work in the city, but I don't live in it. It's mainly a place to crash and eat."

She worried her bottom lip for a few seconds before asking the question that had been on her mind since the previous night. "So, home is the house? You and Benito share it?"

The smile faded, replaced by a look she couldn't quite interpret. "We co-own it." Which didn't tell her anything. But she let the subject and the conversation drop, drawing back a little in self-preservation.

Dante parked in front of an old building and let her into an apartment on the second floor. It practically screamed single, unattached man.

Huge, casual couch. Weight bench with a collection of weight disks. A ten-speed bike on a stationary exercise stand.

All in a semicircle around a big-screen TV.

Dante waved in the direction of a paper-loaded desk positioned a few feet away from a bed at the back of the room. "Help yourself to the computer. A bacon, lettuce, tomato sandwich okay with you?"

On cue, Calista's stomach tightened and her mouth watered. One bagel and a light dinner the night before, combined with vigorous sex, had left her hungrier than she realized.

"That's fine," she said, moving to the desk and turning the computer on. She didn't expect to find anything relevant to the case, and she didn't, but she did find confirmation that her instincts were correct. The egg-selling business was alive and flourishing, and anyone expecting to adopt the kind of child Jessica would have produced could expect to spend well upwards of fifty thousand dollars in "fees" and "expense reimbursements".

Dante joined her a few minutes later, carefully relocating the piles of papers so they didn't mingle, before setting a plate with two sandwiches down and asking, "What do you want to drink?"

"Soda's fine. Diet if you've got it."

"Yeah. I've got some Diet Coke on hand."

He came back with a Coke for her and water for him. When they finished eating, Dante surfed through the various sites she'd been looking at, including some San Francisco fertility clinics that seemed to specialize in acquiring and offering suitable egg donations. A few minutes later he pulled up a page showing a distinguished-looking doctor and started cursing.

She leaned in to read the name. Dr. Robert Lassiter. It didn't mean anything to her, but apparently it did to Dante. "You know him?"

Dante leaned back in his chair and closed his eyes. "Not personally. His wife is Kathy Mitchell. Sister of Eric. Aunt of John."

The boy Dante shot and killed.

Calista took a fresh look at the piles of paper on Dante's desk. More than one of them had the name Mitchell on it. "You're worried about…" His eyes snapped open. She tried again. "All the cops in my family say it was a righteous kill."

He leaned forward abruptly. "It was, but that doesn't mean shit to families like the Mitchells. Hell, they've already started a smear campaign." He leaned back in his chair again and closed his eyes. "If you knew what was good for you, you'd stay away from me."

She was helpless against the pain and anger she saw in him—the hurt. "I think it may be too late for that," she whispered, offering the only comfort she thought he'd willingly accept. She stood, placing a hand on his chest as she leaned down and brushed her lips against his, tentatively at first, then with more confidence as he opened his mouth and met her tongue with his, coaxing it into his mouth, rubbing and twining against it until they were both out of breath.

"You're so sweet, Lista," he murmured when they broke apart, "so beautiful. Take off your clothes and let me look at you."

Chapter Eight

Color rushed to her face and she looked to the window, grateful that a gauzy curtain allowed the light in but granted some privacy. Dante shifted in his seat, drawing her attention instantly back to him, and she knew instinctively that if she didn't comply, he would punish her.

She shivered, not afraid of being punished but not wanting it without Benito present—at least not until she was surer of Dante, of what it meant to him, to them. Her fingers trembled slightly as she removed her shirt and jeans, and her heart cried with pleasure at what she read in his face.

He leaned forward, as though he couldn't help himself, cupping her bra-covered breast and rubbing his thumb over her nipple. "You like that, don't you, baby? You like being petted and admired."

She clamped her legs together in reaction to his words, to the need that had her labia swelling and her clit pressing against her panties as her underwear grew wet. "Yes," she whispered, barely recognizing her own voice.

His hand dropped away from her breast and she wanted to cry out. "Take the rest of it off and I'll give you what you need."

She unclasped the bra and let it slide off her arms and drop to the floor before she did the same with her panties. This time she remembered to wait for him to tell her to remove the shoes, so he wouldn't punish her as he'd promised he'd do.

She felt both powerless and powerful standing in front of him—naked except for the high heels, submissive—while he remained clothed and in control. And yet the look of masculine satisfaction and possessiveness on his face, the sight of his erection pressing aggressively against his jeans made her feel so feminine, so desirable, so utterly…loved…that she knew she'd never be happy in a relationship that didn't include this.

He stood and led her to the bed, stopping at the corner and pulling her against his still-clothed body as his hands stroked down her back and over her buttocks. She tensed when his fingers trailed along the cleft of her ass, and fought the instinctive urge to clamp her cheeks together as Benito's words whispered through her mind. *You need to get used to this, Lista. You need to get used to having a man this way. Dante and I are both going to want to fuck you here. And then we're going to want to fuck you at the same time. One of us in your sweet little pussy and the other in your tight little ass.*

"Get on the bed, baby," Dante said, stepping back so she could obey. "On your back, with your knees bent and your legs spread."

She complied, blushing at the picture she made with her high heels still on and her inner thighs glistening wet with arousal as she held herself open so he could look. His gaze roamed over her body, finally settling on her cunt. And she couldn't keep a small whimper from escaping.

Dante knelt on the bed then and rubbed his fingers through her slit, collecting the moisture and swirling it around her clit and then moving downward, over her virgin back entrance. She tightened, trying to shield the area by pressing her buttocks together, and his hand returned to her smooth pussy, giving her a small warning slap.

"This is what it means to belong to us, Lista," he said, covering her mound with his hand and trapping the heat of his blow between her bare flesh and his palm. "It means everything is ours," his fingers moved downward again, the tips resting on the small pucker of her anus, "including this. We'll both take you here, and once we've gotten you ready, then we'll take you at the same time—one of us squeezed into your hot little cunt while the other one fills your ass."

She whimpered and kept herself from denying him access as his fingers explored, brushing across the small rosette, pressing against it until it relaxed. "That's it, baby, trust me to know what I'm doing. To get you ready." He leaned over and rubbed his cheek against her pussy before giving her a series of small, sucking, biting kisses that had her arching, desperate for him to reach her clit, to slide his tongue in her channel.

"Please, Dante," she begged.

His laugh was husky against her heated flesh. He pressed one last kiss to her skin before standing and removing his clothing.

Calista was shaking all over—with nerves, with arousal, with anticipation, with a need so deep it scared her. She couldn't take her eyes off him. Couldn't stop herself from whimpering when he removed a tube of lubricant from the nightstand and then settled on the bed next to her, running his hand along her inner thighs.

"Let's take these off of you now, baby," he whispered, his hand slipping down first one calf and then the other so he could remove her high heels. "You were a good girl to leave them on. Now remember to keep your knees up and your legs spread, Lista. I'd rather reward you right now than punish you." His palm slipped between her thighs once again.

"Please," she whispered again, not sure how much more she could stand.

He smiled and leaned over, kissing her as his fingers toyed with her clit, making her whimper and arch into his hand.

She found his penis, wet with his own excitement, and brushed her thumb across its tip. He groaned and shifted so her fingers could wrap around his shaft and slide up and down.

Christ. He wasn't sure how much he was in control.

He should have pulled away when she touched his cock, should have punished her then told her to play with her nipples. But her hand felt so good he wanted to tell her to guide him to her cunt opening and stay there while he tunneled inside her.

Fuck. He needed to finish what he'd started. He needed to get her ready so he and Benito could take her at the same time. Nothing felt as good as taking a woman like that.

His cock jerked as her thumb ran over its head again. Christ, he was lying to himself. Yeah, he wanted her with Benito, but looking at her, petting her, fucking her—everything about Calista satisfied him.

It took every bit of control he had to position himself between her legs without burying himself in her slick channel. "I want you to put your hands on my shoulders, now," he said, his cock screaming in protest when she removed her hand.

He opened the lubricant, squeezing it generously on his fingers and his cock before saying, "Don't tense up and don't try to keep me out. I don't want to have to stop and punish you. Okay?" When she nodded, he smiled and leaned over to rub his lips against hers. "Good girl. You know Benito's going to be proud of you, don't you?"

She nodded, primitive fear and complete acceptance in her eyes, and Dante felt like a hot wire was running from his heart to his dick. *You're getting in too deep,* his mind screamed. But it was already too late, he couldn't have pulled himself back if he'd wanted to.

With a groan, his fingers slid between her butt cheeks, zeroing in on her virgin ass, opening her, preparing her for his cock. He held off as long as he could, until he knew that if he didn't work his way into her soon, he wasn't going to make it past the first squeeze of her tight muscles against the head of his cock.

He guided himself to her tight little entrance, watching her face as he slowly worked himself in. Her emotional tears tore him up, but the flush of her arousal and the acceptance in her gaze put him back together again, changing him in ways he wasn't willing to think about, not now, not when he needed to move, to fuck in and out of her.

He leaned down and kissed her tears away. Her lips found his, needing further reassurance, and he gave it to her, rubbing her tongue with his before pulling away and whispering, "Okay now?"

She nodded and he began moving, slowly at first, easing her into the rhythm, rewarding her with the brush of his pelvis over her clit on each in-stroke, until finally her cries of pleasure and her sob of release caused him to lose control, to pump hard and fast, his own climax so violent it left him shuddering and panting above her.

His head was spinning and his heart was roaring. He wanted to collapse on the bed, but he needed to take care of her. Hell, he *wanted* to take care of her.

Christ, this was bad. He should have let Benito get her ready.

His cock pulsed in protest and she whimpered at the movement, at the possibility he was going to take her again. "It's okay, baby, I know you're not ready to do this again right now. We're going to go take a shower, then we can take a nap before we swing by Jessica's apartment building and head back to the house." When she might have protested, he gave her a quick kiss. "We've both been up all night and we'll both be more alert and better able to think about your case with a little sleep."

Somehow he found the strength to pull out of her, to lead her to the shower. It wasn't meant for two people, but the tightness forcing her so close that their bodies continually touched didn't bother him, and he couldn't stop himself from ordering her to wrap her legs around him while he took her again under a hot spray of water.

Afterward they crawled under the covers and he pulled her against him, his hand wedging automatically between her thighs, covering her bare pussy as he spooned around her. Christ, he'd never done this with a woman after any kind of sex, never even wanted to. Yeah, they clung to him, or snuggled up, and after a good fuck he *let* them do it, figuring he owed them that much—but this was completely different. He rubbed his hand over her smooth flesh and her clit immediately stiffened, stabbing into his palm, though Calista mumbled, already asleep.

Masculine satisfaction and pride surged through him, along with another, shakier emotion—one he didn't want to explore. He closed his eyes, forcing his mind away from where this was heading and what was going to happen when they got there. It was too late now, had probably been too late from the moment he'd seen her walk into the bar with Lyric. It had definitely been too late as soon as he'd seen Benito go in without a condom and then he'd gone in the same way. His cock jerked in anticipation but his heart jumped in panic.

Fuck. The fact that neither of them had asked her about birth control told him something he wasn't ready to hear.

He buried his face in her hair and concentrated on the heat of her body, on how much he liked the smooth flesh between her thighs. Christ, he wasn't sure he'd like it any other way now. She was so damn beautiful. Inside and outside. Perfect. He could hardly wait to take her at the same time Benito did.

* * * * *

Calista woke first and was glad she'd given in and taken a nap. She grinned thinking about exactly why she'd needed one so badly, then frowned when she eased out from under the covers and realized how tender she was between her legs. She hadn't been with anyone for a long time, and between Benito and Dante...between last night and that last bout of lovemaking in the shower...

Disappointment and a flash of worry washed through her. They were probably used to women who could fuck an army and still be able to take on the Marines.

She bit her lip in silent reprimand. That wasn't fair. Just because she hated the idea of them being with other women, it didn't give her the right to put those other women down.

Sighing, she put her clothes back on and picked up the case file before slipping out of Dante's apartment. She wanted to make some phone calls without waking him. She also needed to put some distance between Dante and her, and what had happened earlier. She was honest enough with herself to admit it.

She was falling hard and she didn't seem to have any defenses when it came to the Giancotti brothers. Even worse, she didn't want to protect herself from them. She wanted this to be...real...not some fantasy interlude that would come to an end and break her heart when it did.

Maybe it was time to take refuge in the case, to concentrate on doing the best job possible for Bulldog and for Sarah Winston, even though she had a feeling this case wasn't going to give Sarah a happy ending or a pleasant closure.

Calista descended to the parking area, glad there was no wind so she could open the case file on the hood of Dante's Jeep. Two questions popped up almost immediately. Where was Jessica's car? And why wasn't there a key for it on the ring with the apartment key?

True, lots of people didn't bother owning cars if they lived in San Francisco. Parking was miserable and expensive, and you could get anywhere you wanted by using mass transit or walking. But she'd bet money Jessica had a car. Someone who was so careful about not leaving anything in her apartment she couldn't walk away from wouldn't have left herself to the mercy of mass transit.

Calista dialed Sarah Winston's Georgia number, and after giving her name to the efficient, businesslike woman who answered the phone, she was put through to Sarah.

"I've only got a moment," Sarah warned when she came on the line. "I've got guests here."

"That's fine, I've just got a quick question. Did you make arrangements for Jessica's car to be sold?"

"If my daughter had a car, I don't know anything about it."

"So the police didn't give you a car key when they released Jessica's possessions."

"There were no keys at all. The key I gave you was provided by the manager."

Calista frowned and started to ask if the police had said anything about the lack of a house key, then held back. Obviously they hadn't—or if they had, they hadn't viewed it as suspicious. "Thanks. I'll let you get back to your guests."

She closed her cellular and reread the report, this time looking at the inventoried list of Jessica's possessions. There were no keys listed. There was also no cell phone.

Calista ran her thumb along the edge of her own phone. Jessica wouldn't have been without a phone. Hell, even some of her kindergarten students had tried to bring them to school!

Maybe Jessica had left it in her car. Or maybe it had gotten separated from the body when she fell.

Calista pulled out the autopsy report. No sign of defense wounds. Cause of death consistent with an accidental fall from a height of a hundred feet — approximate distance from the tenth floor. Consumption of alcohol and drugs most likely contributed to victim having impaired judgment and/or losing balance.

She read further, this time paying attention to what they'd found in Jessica's blood and tissue samples. Alcohol .05 percent, so not necessarily drunk, though probably intoxicated. Ecstasy. That wasn't a surprise. Calista could imagine what Jessica was thinking and feeling. The baby was delivered and she was heading for Hawaii. It was time to party — to act like a twenty-three-year-old with money in the bank and life by the tail. No more attorneys and doctors telling her what to do. She was free to have fun.

Calista was willing to bet drug tests were part of the deal. So Jessica had probably been clean for a while, at least for the last nine months and maybe earlier if she'd started out by selling her eggs. Maybe she'd underestimated the impact of the drugs on her system.

There was a final drug listed. Flunitrazepam — more commonly known as Rohypnol.

She frowned. The name sounded familiar. Then again, between all the cops in her family and all the teacher-training seminars she'd attended on drugs and drug use, she could have heard the name Rohypnol anywhere.

Her thoughts returned to Jessica's missing car and for a split second she was tempted to wait and have Dante look into it. But before the idea could settle in, she blocked it and called Tyler instead.

"Hey, doll, how's the case going?" She told him what she'd come up with so far and was rewarded by his impressed whistle. "Nice work."

"Which is why I'm calling you. Do you think you can dig around in the DMV records and see if she had a car?"

"I assume you don't want just a yes or no answer to that question."

She couldn't help but smile. Compared to the men in her family, Tyler was so easygoing. "I'm glad you're cutting me some slack since I'm kind of making this up as I go along."

"Hey, everyone has a first case, and you're acting like an old pro."

"How soon can you check on the car?"

He laughed. "See what I mean about being a pro? You're already putting a time limit on getting an answer to your question."

"In a nice, not a pushy way."

He laughed again. "I can probably get back to you by the end of the day. Right now I'm heading out for a while. If I don't get tied up in the field, I'll tackle it when I get back. Otherwise I'll come in and do it tomorrow morning. Sounds like you're stuck unless the apartment manager or the other tenants can tell you something, so I'll do my best."

"Thanks, Tyler." She gave him Jessica's information and was about to hang up when she thought about the drug name. "Hey, Jessica had Flunitrazepam, with a notation that says it's more commonly known as Rohypnol, in her system. Sound familiar?"

"Sure, doll. It got its fame as a date-rape drug. On the street it's also known as roofies. Causes dizziness, confusion, loss of consciousness, loss of muscle control, and the victim often can't remember what happened to them." He paused for a minute. "You got the autopsy report in front of you?"

"Yes."

"Any indication of sexual assault or recent sexual activity?"

"None. I noticed that yesterday when I first read the report. So maybe someone slipped it into her drink, but she wandered away or it took effect before they thought it would."

"Could be. Like I said, it's mainly a date-rape drug, but some users claim it extends their alcohol buzz and makes the high from other drugs even higher. So it's possible she took it on her own."

"She had a blood-alcohol of .05 percent and ecstasy in her system."

"There you have it. Without knowing more about her, it's too early to say for sure that someone was planning on having her star in their own sick little party. It would also explain why she might have gone over the balcony."

Dante appeared at the bottom of the stairs, the concern on his face swiftly moving into a frown when he saw her.

"Thanks, Tyler," Calista said, "I gotta run."

"Me too, doll. Talk to you later."

Chapter Nine

Calista pocketed the phone and closed the file before moving toward Dante. She'd seen the same look on her father's and her brothers' faces a thousand times—worry with nowhere to go but into temper. She pressed against Dante and gave him a kiss before he could speak. "I didn't want to wake you up," she said between the first kiss and the second.

He grunted, mollified, and pulled her against him before deepening the kiss and reestablishing who was in charge. "You get a call back?" he asked when the kiss ended.

"No, just talking to Tyler."

Dante's eyebrows drew together in the start of a frown and she almost laughed at how predictable he was. God, he was just like the men in her family. It was so obvious now she didn't know why she'd missed it—strike that. She did not think about letting the men in her family do the things to her Dante did.

"It was about the case," she said. "Speaking of which, do you have stuff you've got to take care of here before we leave?"

"I've got to check for messages and lock up."

She followed him back into the apartment and washed their lunch dishes while he used the phone. When he was finished, they headed out, and she could tell by the way he was backtracking their earlier route that he remembered her desire to swing by Jessica's apartment complex before leaving San Francisco.

She hadn't had time to call ahead to see if the apartment manager was there or not, but it didn't really matter, not if they were going to stop anyway. This time they had to park a little further away and walk, but Calista still counted herself lucky when she saw a woman dressed in funk-trendy clothing unlocking the door between Jessica's apartment and the manager's.

"Excuse me," Calista called out, relieved when the woman actually looked in her direction and kept standing rather than bolt into her apartment and lock the door.

Calista hurried over and introduced herself. The woman, Amy, said, "You're the one that left the card. It freaked me out, my neighbor being investigated and all. I thought she died in a weird accident." Amy shivered. "Spooky, going over a railing and diving ten stories."

Calista was glad now that she'd already figured out what she was going to say. "As far as I know it was an accident. Mainly her parents are looking for some closure. They were estranged from Jessica and now they want to know what the last couple years of her life were like."

"Oh, gotcha. Yeah. I can see that. Sorry, not sure I can help. She and I weren't friends or anything. Mainly we only knew each other in passing."

"Did she have friends who came around a lot?"

"Not a lot. But the last three or four months there were a couple of girls." Amy's nose wrinkled up. "They were young and pregnant too. I think they may have worked at the same place she did. Did her parents know she had a baby?"

"Yes. I assume she put it up for adoption?"

Amy shrugged. "No idea. Probably. I mean, she was single and I never heard a baby crying, so I don't think she came home with it. Well, the truth is, the last month or so, she's hardly been here at all. I maybe saw her once, and since she didn't mention having the baby, I didn't ask about it."

"Any idea where Jessica worked?"

"No. Somewhere she had to wear nice clothes. And I think maybe it was part time, because she didn't go out dressed for work every day."

"Any boyfriends?"

"Not that I know of, but I've only lived here for about seven months. So if you're wondering who the father of the baby was, I don't have a clue."

"What about the people in the upstairs apartments? Was she friendly with them?"

Amy snorted. "Not likely."

Calista bit down on her bottom lip as her mind raced to make sure she'd covered all the important questions. The only thing she hadn't asked about was the car. "Do you know if Jessica had a car?"

"Oh yeah. Sure. A siren-red Mustang." She frowned. "Now that you mention it, I haven't seen it around for a month, maybe longer."

Dante joined them and Amy's eyebrows drew together as her attention moved to him. "Hey, are you in the movies or something? Your face looks familiar."

"Or something."

Calista said, "Could I get a phone number, just in case I think of anything else?"

Amy rattled off a number and said, "It's my cell."

Which made Calista ask, "Did you ever see Jessica with a cell phone?"

"Yeah. Sure. I mean, who *doesn't* have a cell phone?"

"Thanks," Calista said, "I appreciate you taking the time to answer my questions. If you remember anything…"

"No problem. I'll give you a call. I've got your card."

Calista started to turn away when Amy pointed. "That's the apartment manager, Mr. Olson, coming up the sidewalk. Today's bingo day down at the Senior Center. If you've been looking for him, that's where he's been." She grimaced. "I've heard he's really, really popular with the ladies at the Center—which is pretty depressing, knowing that even when we're old ladies there still won't be enough men to go around. I'm not sure how much he's home, or how well he knew Jessica, but he might be worth talking to."

"Thanks," Calista said again before moving to intercept Mr. Olson.

His eyes widened with recognition when he saw Dante, and for an instant she thought he looked afraid. But then he turned his attention to her and listened to her rehearsed story before saying, "Yes, I talked to her mother. Poor woman. I'm sorry. I can't tell you anything I didn't already tell Mrs. Winston. Jessica kept to herself, paid her rent on time. She didn't have any complaints and I didn't get any complaints about her. So I'm afraid I didn't have very much to do with her."

"Do you know who she worked for?"

"Can't say that I do."

Calista frowned. True, she hadn't rented very many apartments, but she'd always had to provide employment and credit information. And even *she* knew that finding housing in San Francisco was tough. "Wouldn't it be on her rental application?"

"Could be, but I don't handle who gets to rent and who doesn't. I just keep an eye on things here and at a few other houses in the neighborhood, heading off problems and making sure the maintenance is kept up with, that kind of thing."

"Who handles the rental applications then?"

Mr. Olson's eyes shifted to Dante again, and this time there was no mistaking the nervousness. "I guess it's public information. The Mitchell Family Trust owns the building, but I don't deal with them directly anymore. Haven't in years, not since Warren Mitchell ran things. He's the one who hired me on about twenty years ago to look after things in exchange for not paying rent." His hand shook just a little bit as he smoothed down his collar.

"They've got a law firm with a real estate department for handling trust client buildings. They handle everything. Gellis & Associates is their name." He licked his lips. "Like I said, it's public information. The few times they've advertised an apartment here, they've given the law firm's phone number. So I don't think I'm violating anyone's trust by telling you. Now if you'll excuse me, I need to get ready for company."

Calista let him go without trying to ask him further questions. His fear of saying something that might cause him to lose his home struck at her core even as the information he'd provided had her heart racing and her mind whirling with possibilities.

She risked a quick glance at Dante. His expression was hard, unyielding, determined, and she had a feeling he'd just become entrenched in her case. "I'm going to see if anyone's home upstairs," she said.

"I'll wait in the car."

Her business cards were still on the doors of the upstairs apartments, which didn't surprise or disappoint Calista. From what Amy said, these tenants were a long shot anyway.

She returned to the car and wrote down what she'd learned as Dante guided the car out of the city and onto the highway.

"I don't think it's a coincidence that Jessica lives in an apartment owned by the Mitchell Family Trust, which just happens to have a fertility doctor specializing in egg donations in the family," she said when she'd finished writing. "Do you think the lawyers handling the rental property will give me any information on Jessica?"

Dante's hands tightened on the steering wheel. "They won't give you shit and I'll probably end up with a call from Internal Affairs tomorrow asking me why I was on one of the Mitchells' properties hassling one of their employees."

Calista reached over and put a hand on his thigh. "You can tell IA to call me. I'll explain what happened."

His hand moved to cover hers. "Don't worry about it. It'll just be the Mitchells hassling me through their lawyers."

"You really think Mr. Olson will call the lawyers? He seemed so…nervous."

"Yeah, he'll call. The more he thinks about it getting back to them and maybe to the Mitchells, the more paranoid he'll get. The only way he'll be able to stop worrying is to confess what he's done."

"It's all public information, right? He won't lose his housing, will he?"

"He'll be okay. Refusing to tell us would have really gotten our attention. And yeah, a couple of calls and we would have known anyway."

Calista worried her bottom lip and wondered if Dante even realized he was saying "we". They lapsed into silence and she looked out the window, hyperaware of how good it felt to have her hand trapped under his.

She liked it too much. She liked being with him too much.

It felt natural, right. The same way it'd felt with Benito almost instantly.

She shivered and a wave of longing washed over her. A need to be wrapped in Benito's arms.

Her heart raced ahead of her thoughts for a second, but her thoughts caught up, warning her once again that she was falling hard and she didn't seem to have any defenses when it came to them. She broke the silence by saying, "I need to go home and take care of my dogs." She smoothed a nonexistent wrinkle on her pants and blushed when she caught Dante watching her. "Maybe we could meet at a restaurant for dinner, then I could take my own car so no one would have to drive me home afterward."

She knew Benito had intended for her to stay the night again, and she'd wanted to, but now... She was still sore. That was reason enough, but it wasn't the real reason she was suggesting dinner in a neutral place. She was already starting to need Benito and Dante too much. Not one or the other, but both of them.

A muscle ticced in Dante's cheek but he didn't say anything. Instead he opened his cellular and called Benito.

"You on your way back?" Benito asked as soon as he answered the call.

"Yeah."

"How'd it go?"

"Calista's case looks like it's going to touch the Mitchells in a couple of places."

"That's bad news."

"Tell me about it." Dante cut a quick look to Calista. "We're on our way to her place. She's got to take care of her dogs, then she wants to meet us at a restaurant for dinner."

"Something happened?"

"Not that I know of."

"You took her to your apartment?"

"Yeah."

"And?"

"What do you think?"

"You fucked her."

"Yeah."

"And she was okay with it?"

"Seemed to be."

"So why does she want to meet at a restaurant instead of coming over here and spending Friday night with us?"

"I don't know."

There was a long sigh at the other end of the phone. "You're not making this easy, bro."

Dante grunted. "You're better at figuring out this stuff than I am."

"And you're a cop. You read people for a living, so what's going on with her?"

Dante looked again and caught her worrying the fabric of her pants, an anxious little gesture that always shot right through him and made him want to pull her into his arms and protect her from everything, even phantom worries.

Hell. "You talk to her." He handed off the phone.

"Hi, sweetheart," Benito said and Calista's chest expanded with the warmth of his voice.

"Hi."

"Everything okay?"

"Yes. I made a lot of headway on the case today. I can tell you about it over dinner."

"It's been okay having Dante with you?"

Calista's face flamed with heat and color as images of what had happened at her house and at his apartment flashed through her mind. "Yes."

"What do you want to do about dinner?"

"I thought we could meet at a restaurant," she said, but her resolve to put some distance between her and the two of them weakened. Her body felt tight and anxious at the thought of being with Benito and not being held and kissed and petted. He was so physical, always touching her and making her feel feminine and adored. "Or if you want, you could pick something up and we could eat at my place."

There was a pause, like she'd surprised him with her offer. But almost immediately he said, "I was thinking Italian. That okay with you?"

"Perfect, I love Italian."

He laughed. "Okay, give me your address and then let me talk to Dante again."

She passed the phone off after telling Benito where she lived. He and Dante talked for a minute more, mainly about timing and what food to order, and then all too soon she was home.

"Not much in the watchdog department," Dante said as they walked in to a quiet house.

Calista laughed. "They're old guys. Even when they hear something, it takes them a few minutes to respond. I've got a doggie door in the kitchen, they're probably out in the sun."

Dante followed her to the kitchen, entranced by the way she moved. Christ, she was so soft and feminine, so different from the women he usually got involved with—hell, fucked—a night of causal sex was not the same as being involved.

His penis pulsed even as his gut tightened against a wave of panic. Shit. She scared him. What she was doing to him scared him.

He forced himself to look away from her and get control, but even that backfired, sending more blood to his already straining cock as images of what it meant to take control *of her* flooded through his mind. Fuck, he hoped Benito got here soon. He needed a buffer between Calista and him.

She opened the kitchen door and stepped out into the backyard. Dante stopped in the doorway and took in the small, well-kept lawn, the wind chimes and hummingbird feeders. Two of her dogs were curled together on a low lounge chair. The third was stretched out on a rocked walkway like roadkill. None of them moved until she was close enough to touch them. *Yeah, not much in the watchdog department.*

A knock sounded at the front door and he retraced his steps, opening it for his brother and saying, "Kitchen's straight through. You got anything else in your truck?"

"Yeah, front seat. I brought a couple of DVDs too. She got a player?"

"Don't know. She's in the backyard." Dante moved past Benito and headed down the walkway.

Benito took a minute to look around the living room, smiling when he spotted the DVD player, then laughing softly when he took in the pictures on her walls, the shelves loaded with Tinkertoys and Legos, Play-Doh and crayons. It fit her so perfectly—and suddenly he couldn't wait to hold her in his arms. Christ. The day had dragged.

He arrived at the kitchen just as she was ushering three miniature dachshunds in from the yard. Her eyes widened with pleasure and his heart expanded at the happiness he saw on her face.

Setting the bags he was carrying down on the kitchen table, he pulled her to him and covered her mouth with his, stroking his tongue in and out, telling her with his kiss just how much he'd missed her during the day.

She clung to him, returning the kiss with soft whimpers and the press of her body against his, telling him without words she'd been thinking of him too.

When they broke apart he said, "I picked up the phone a hundred times and started to call. But I didn't have your cell number...and I didn't want to interrupt your time with Dante." He kissed her again. "You and Dante were okay together?"

Her face flamed and she ducked her head. "Yes."

Benito laughed, knowing from the heat in her face and her expression that whatever had happened between her and his brother had been intense, and had probably involved Dante being very dominant and her being very submissive. Benito rubbed his hand against her cheek before cupping her face and lifting it so their eyes met. He leaned down and gave her a butterfly kiss on the lips. "It makes me happy to think about you two together."

One of the little dogs started barking, a strange coughing sound, and Calista pulled out of Benito's arms and said, "That's his 'hurry up and feed me' bark."

Dante walked in with a few more bags and set them on the table. "He coughing up a hairball?"

Calista laughed. "Cats cough up hairballs, not dogs."

"So what's wrong with his bark?" Benito asked.

"Somewhere along the line someone had him debarked and this is what's left. In fact, all three of my old guys are debarked." She shrugged. "I've never had dachshunds before. My family has always gone for big dogs, German Shepherds mainly, and Rottweilers. But one of the dachshund rescue ladies told me dachshunds can be terrible barkers and for apartment and condo dwellers, it sometimes comes down to a choice between moving, getting rid of the dog or having it debarked."

"What are their names?" Benito asked.

"The guy in the green collar is Chance, the one in the yellow is Lucky, and T-Rex has the red collar."

Benito's smile widened. Chance and Lucky he could see—but T-Rex? Not in this lifetime.

She caught the smile and the gist of his thoughts and gave him a teacher frown. "It's not the outside that matters, it's what's on the inside."

Benito laughed. "Yeah, but T-Rex? As in Tyrannosaurus Rex?"

"He's got a giant heart. He was almost dead when Lyric rescued him." Calista pulled out a can of dog food and opened it, shooting Dante and Benito a quizzical look. "Did you guys have pets when you were kids?"

Dante's expression tightened immediately and she knew instantly that their childhood was a closed subject, at least with him. Even Benito's face was more somber than usual, but he answered the question. "No. No pets."

She let the subject drop, turning her attention to feeding the dogs, then to moving the bags from the kitchen table to the counter so she could set the table. Benito and Dante moved to her side, helping her unpack the food.

Calista nibbled at her bottom lip, wishing now that she'd had time to change before Benito arrived. She'd wanted to put on a dress. Yeah, she knew it was silly and hopelessly…old-fashioned…romantic…but…

"What's wrong?" Benito asked, surprising her with his attentiveness.

"Nothing." She couldn't stop her cheeks from warming. "I just wanted to change into something else before you got here."

His smile sent her heart stumbling and tripping in her chest. "Go change then. Dante and I can set the table and put the food out." He pressed a quick kiss to her mouth. "But don't take too long or there won't be anything left to eat. We take our food seriously."

She laughed and surveyed all the food he'd brought with him, along with the drinks, two DVDs, and some microwave popcorn. "Looks like you've got enough to camp out for the weekend."

He grinned. "Wishful thinking."

"Yours or mine?"

"Both, I hope."

She leaned in and kissed him. "I'll be right back."

Calista hurried to the bedroom, glad she already knew what dress she wanted to wear, glad also that she'd showered at Dante's earlier. Her eyes strayed to the huge bed—Lyric, Cady, and Erin's housewarming gift—and she wondered if Dante and Benito would be willing to stay with her tonight, even if she was too sore to go as far as they'd like.

She moved to the closet and took out a patterned sundress she knew brought out the blue in her eyes and made her tan look darker. For tonight, she left her bra off, knowing on another day, when she wasn't too sore for sex, she'd also leave the panties off.

A quick brush of her hair and she was ready to go back out. She counted herself fortunate that her eyelashes were already thick and black and her skin was good so she rarely bothered putting on makeup.

Calista took one last look in the mirror, smiling ruefully at herself. *The men in your family have sure trained you well.*

Pants, even nice ones, never received a compliment. But dresses and skirts…it was almost embarrassing how even the most rowdy of her brothers, cousins or uncles was suddenly opening doors, pulling out chairs and fussing over how beautiful she was—well, in all fairness— how beautiful any Burke female was, from five years old to ninety-five, as long as they were in a dress or skirt.

She returned to the kitchen and was immediately met by Dante's low whistle and Benito's hug along with his, "You're beautiful, Lista."

"Thanks." She hugged him back before turning to survey the table. They had everything on it, including wine glasses full of wine. "You want me to put some music on?"

Dante grinned. "You'd have to be the tiebreaker. I like rock but since Benito bought his pickup truck, he's moved to country."

Calista laughed and wrinkled her nose. "I'm not sure how good a tiebreaker I'll be. I like both." She nibbled her bottom lip for a second then sighed, going over to give Dante a kiss. "That's a consolation prize. I think I'm in the mood for Alan Jackson tonight."

He pulled her up against him, giving her a deeper kiss before letting her go. "I'll take the consolation prize any day. And for the record, I don't hate country — except when Benito's singing along."

"Be right back."

She turned the music on in the living room but kept it low enough so they could talk over dinner — which they did, about everything from the case to Benito's stories about his Las Vegas clients and the major headache of providing status bodyguards for A-list wannabes. Afterward they moved into the living room. Dante plopped on the couch. Benito took the comfortably padded chair, pulling her onto his lap. When she made a murmur of protest, he curled her against his body and said, "He had you all day, now it's my turn."

His hand slid up and down her thigh, moving underneath her dress and causing her clit to beg hungrily for attention. She rubbed her cheek against his and whimpered when his fingers toyed with the waistband of her panties. But before he could slip them inside, she grabbed his wrist through her clothing.

"Are you sore, sweetheart?"

"Yes."

His hand moved around to her back and lower, cupping her ass cheeks. When she tensed, he rubbed his nose along hers. "There too?"

"A little bit." Her answer was barely audible.

He nuzzled against her cheek, burying his face in her hair and sucking her earlobe into his mouth as his hand stroked her buttocks. "Did you like it when Dante fucked you there?"

"Yes."

His tongue traced the shell of her ear before slipping into the delicate, ultra-sensitive channel.

Calista cried out, her nipples going hard and tight as her body arched. Benito's free hand brushed the straps of the sundress off her shoulders before pushing the dress down and cupping her breast.

"I can't," she whispered.

"I know, sweetheart. Just let me pet you. Let me show you how happy I am you let Dante love you like that."

He tweaked her nipple in time to the sensuous tongue thrusts into her ear. His low moans and the feel of his erection against her bottom making her shiver.

Dante moved over in front of her, cupping her other breast and taking its fiercely aroused tip into his mouth, his lips and tongue and teeth giving her so much pleasure that her fingers speared through his hair as she pressed against him, wanting him to swallow her whole.

Fire raced to her clit and she cried out, overwhelmed by the sensation, by their attention. Benito's fingers moved along the band of her panties, then slipped inside, covering her clit and she was lost, unable to do anything other than yield completely, to give herself up to them as explosive pleasure consumed her.

She felt as limp as a rag doll afterward, boneless and weak. Benito's hands moved to her hair and to her belly, stroking her as he murmured words of praise and slowly brought her back to herself. Dante eased the straps of her dress back up over her shoulders before he kissed her and returned to the couch. Her eyes followed him, taking in the erection and the harsh need on his face.

Benito's swollen cock pressed against her buttocks and when she moved, he stiffened and gave a shaky little breath that sent a thrill of pleasure through her. Her eyes left Dante and she moved her head so she could brush her lips against Benito's. "Let me take care of you now," she whispered, already sliding off his lap.

His body tensed as she opened his pants. Without a word he moved to the edge of the chair, helped her ease his clothing down and free his cock. She knelt in front of him, tracing the muscles in his thighs as her hands moved toward his straining penis, as she admired the beauty of him.

When her hand reached its destination, he jerked in her fingers and bathed the tip of his cock with his arousal. She swirled her thumb over the head, spreading the silky moisture as her other hand cupped his balls, testing their weight and exploring the smooth skin behind them with the tips of her fingers.

His hands went to her head, burying into her hair. "God, Lista. Put your mouth on me."

She let him guide her face to his cock, let him press it between her parted lips. But she didn't start sucking until her teeth and tongue had driven him higher, to the point where his body was shaking and he was begging, pleading with her. And then she sucked, hard pulls that had his buttocks clenching and his body arching until finally he cried out in release.

Calista lingered for a minute, enjoying the way he was stroking her hair and telling her how good she was, how much he'd liked that. Only slowly did she withdraw.

Her gaze moved to Dante and a fresh wave of feminine power rushed through her at the sight of his fingers wrapped around his cock, at the feral hunger on his face. She went to him immediately, kneeling down and looking up at him through her eyelashes, already knowing how his needs were different than Benito's.

"Don't tease me, Lista," he warned. "Suck it now."

She obeyed, taking him into her mouth, working his cock as she had earlier in the day, her heart filling with the sounds of his pleasure as she brought him to orgasm.

Afterward they retrieved the wine and the DVDs from the kitchen. "I didn't know what you liked," Benito said as he moved to stand in front of the TV. "So I brought *Get Shorty* and *Man of Fire*."

"I love *Get Shorty*," Calista said. "Let's start with that one."

Benito turned on the TV as Dante sprawled on the couch. Almost immediately the three dachshunds left their round bed and moved to stand next to the couch, eyes on Dante.

Calista laughed. "The TV going on is their cue that it's snuggle time." She leaned over and rubbed her lips against Dante's. "Do you mind sharing the couch with them?"

How could he deny her? Christ. His head was still spinning from feeling her mouth on his cock, from watching her suck Benito off. "As long as they don't try to hog the couch," he growled and was rewarded with her smile and another kiss.

She picked the dogs up one by one and set them on the couch. "Don't let them jump off. Dachshunds are prone to back injuries. I don't want them to hurt themselves."

Dante had to laugh. She was such a worrier. As far as he could tell, the three old dogs were already stretched out along his body and halfway to being dead to the world. They weren't exactly balls of fire, ready to spring into action at the slightest sound. Hell, he could probably fire a gun next to them and they wouldn't react.

"You're laughing at me," she said and her pout had him pulling her face down to his.

"Just a little bit," he said before kissing her. "Now go sit on Benito's lap like a good girl so we can watch the movie."

Chapter Ten

Calista was already up when Tyler knocked on the door the next morning. "I got in late and you had company." His eyebrows lifted. "And you still have company, but I thought you'd want this. It's the information on the car."

"You found something!"

"Yeah, not sure it'll do you any good. She sold the car about two months ago."

Calista stepped out of the doorway. "Have you had breakfast yet?"

Tyler grinned. "I thought you'd never ask."

She smiled. For all Tyler's talents, cooking wasn't one of them—unless it took place on a grill. "Come on back to the kitchen. I can fix you an omelet, or pancakes if you'd rather have that."

"One of your omelets sounds good. Does a cup of coffee come with it?"

"There's a pot ready now."

Tyler fixed himself a cup of coffee and sat down while Calista went to work on his breakfast. Even knowing she had two men in her bed and they'd eventually wander out, she felt comfortable having Tyler at her kitchen table. She wasn't nervous at all—well, not more than just a little bit—but it wasn't as though he didn't know Dante and Benito were here. Both their cars were parked out front.

And inviting Tyler in for breakfast was not even close to facing off with Kieran or the rest of her brothers.

"Did you make any more headway on your case yesterday?" Tyler asked.

"Some. I was really hoping we'd hit the jackpot with the car." She went on to tell him about the conversation with Amy and Mr. Olson, and the link to the Mitchell family.

Tyler let out a soft whistle. "That's an interesting coincidence. Can't say I like it."

Calista flipped his omelet over and turned the bacon. "Neither do I."

Dante knew he didn't have anything to worry about with Tyler. But Christ...it was making him crazy to lie in bed and listen to her entertaining another man in the kitchen, to hear soft conversation and picture her making Tyler's breakfast.

Fuck! He rolled out of bed and pulled on his jeans, not bothering with his shirt or shoes.

She looked up when he walked in, blushing slightly but not hesitating to move over and place a hand on his bare chest as she brushed a kiss across his mouth. "Tyler's having a cheese-jalapeno-green pepper omelet with bacon on the side. I've also got onions and mushrooms. What do you want?"

Dante's gut tightened. Christ, she was making him need things he'd never had. He and Benito had been fending for themselves their entire lives, making do with casual sex to fill a void that started early on, with the eighteen-year-old drug-addicted mother who gave birth to them but never loved them.

"What he's having is fine." It came out a growl, but she didn't seem to take offense.

"There's coffee, help yourself." She moved back to the stove and transferred Tyler's breakfast to a plate, and then to him, before starting Dante's breakfast.

Dante poured coffee and sat down at the table, watching her work with an odd little ache in his gut. Goddamn, he could get used to this. Waking up to this. He frowned slightly. Well, with the exception of Tyler. He liked the other man, but he wouldn't want to see him across the breakfast table every morning.

Dante's eyes fell on the manila folder and he reached for it, pulling it closer to him. "What's in the folder?"

Calista stiffened but didn't turn around. "Just some research Tyler did for me." Dante's muscles tightened and his cop instincts started buzzing. He flipped the file open and saw the DMV run on Jessica Winston.

He stared at it, wanting to put Calista across his lap and burn her ass with the palm of his hand for trying to cut him out of the case—for not asking him to dig around in the DMV records. Yeah, technically he was on administrative leave, but there were guys he could contact, buddies who would have run this for him.

He gritted his teeth as his cock pressed against his jeans. He'd warned her about holding out on him. Once Tyler was gone...

Benito walked into the kitchen, his hair a wild tangle, his chest and feet bare too. Dante stilled, waiting to see how Calista would react, wondering if she'd pretend she hadn't been with both of them and hurt Benito by acting as though there was nothing between them.

She turned from the stove, smiling at Benito, drawing him to her with the emotion in her face. Benito leaned down, kissing her, lingering until she finally laughed and pushed him away. "You're going to make me burn Dante's breakfast. Get some coffee and sit down, then I'll start on yours."

Benito laughed, kissing her again before making his coffee and sitting at the table. "She must be a good cook to have you visiting this early on a Saturday morning," Benito said to Tyler.

"I'd starve to death if it weren't for Erin and Calista, Cady too before she headed off for Texas."

Calista put Dante's breakfast on a plate and brought it to the table, setting it down in front of him and casually trying to escape with the folder. His hand clamped on her wrist, tightening in warning. "Not a chance, Lista."

Benito reached over, circling Calista's wrist above Dante's hand, tugging gently until his brother let her go. "We can split an omelet so you can sit down and eat," he said, pulling her attention away from his brother and the file.

"I ate before Tyler got here. I wasn't sure how long you guys would stay in bed." Her face warmed with color. "My brothers all sleep in on the days they don't work."

Dante's frown had shifted from her to the contents of the folder. "What's the name on the bank statement Jessica's mother found?"

"Lindsey Smyth," Calista answered.

"According to this, that's who bought her car."

Excitement rushed through Calista and she leaned over to get a look at the papers in the file. "I think that's the same Reno address on the bank statement!"

Tyler shook his head. "Damn. I would have come by last night with the info, but I didn't think it was a big deal." He grinned. "Guess it's a good thing I swung by for breakfast this morning. Maybe I should check in at lunch and dinner time, just to make sure the bases are all covered."

Calista laughed and looked at his empty plate. "Do you want something else, or are you full?"

"One more and I'll do you a favor while you're cooking it."

"Hmmm, what's the favor?"

"I've got a buddy in Reno. I'll call and ask him to do a drive-by, check out this address, maybe even get a few pictures."

"Deal!" Calista said. "And I'll let you read my notes while I fix you another omelet."

Benito noticed the scowl on Dante's face and felt a jolt of excitement and satisfaction. For his brother to be bothered by the exchange between Tyler and Calista meant Dante was hooked—not that Benito was surprised. *God, how could any man not love her?* He frowned at the thought and looked at Tyler, then shrugged it off. Friends. Tyler was the kind of guy who had a million female friends.

Calista started to move away and Benito halted her with an arm around her waist, giving her what he hoped was a suitably pathetic what-about-my-breakfast look. She rewarded him with a laugh and a smile, followed by a quick kiss. "I haven't forgotten you."

Christ. She was so affectionate and loving. So quick to touch him and give him exactly what he needed. It was like having sunshine poured into his soul.

If Tyler wasn't sitting at the table, he'd pull her down on his lap and see if she was still too sore, because right now his heart felt like it was going to burst. He wanted to be inside her, his cock surrounded by her heat, his arms wrapped around her, his lips locked to hers, telling her with his body how much she meant to him. She kissed him again, lingering this time, her eyes soft and shining as they met his for an instant before she escaped his grasp and went into the living room.

Calista returned with a folder and set it on the table, then moved to the stove. Tyler made his call and got one in return as she set Benito's breakfast in front of him.

"Bad news," Tyler said. "The address is one of those places with rental mailboxes where you get a street address and a person who'll sign for packages during business hours. Jerick will go around and see if he can charm some information out of whoever's working. It's a long shot, but he's a lucky guy, so who knows." Tyler closed his cell phone and reached for the case file. "Do I still get seconds?"

"You still get seconds because I'm not done with your help yet. I made some copies of the photo Jessica's mother gave me. It's also scanned into the Crime Tells computer on Cady's desk. Could you e-mail or fax Jerick a copy so he can take it with him when he goes to the mailbox address? She was a beautiful woman. I think people— especially guys—would remember seeing her."

Tyler's eyebrows rose. "You may be on to something, doll. Why buy a new car when you can sell the one you've got to yourself?"

"That's the idea I can't get out of my head, especially after seeing her apartment. She was ready to run, but what good does it do to run under your own name? And why else would she have a bank statement with another name and so much money in it?" Calista's eyebrows drew together. "I can't figure out how it's connected to the baby. Amy said Jessica never brought it home with her, so I don't think she was holding out, trying to get more money for signing over the relinquishment papers."

"Maybe it doesn't involve the baby at all," Benito said.

Calista returned to the stove. "That's almost worse. It'd mean she was involved in something scary and dangerous." Before the words were completely out, her heart started racing, making the next leap, thinking about the Mitchell family, and wondering…just wondering…if Jessica's accident had really been an accident.

She didn't say anything. She didn't need to.

Benito leaned over and looked at Jessica's picture. "Maybe she got done with her stint producing eggs and a baby for Lassiter and hooked up with his nephews."

Calista put Tyler's plate down in front of him and caught Dante's scowl. Uncertain whether it was at her waiting on Tyler or because the case touched the Mitchell family in so many places, she brushed her fingers over his bare shoulder. "Had enough?" His scowl deepened and she decided it'd be safer to add, "To eat. Do you want another omelet?"

"No."

She didn't like the way his answer rubbed across her skin, but she didn't want to push him. Not now. Not in front of Tyler. She got a fresh cup of coffee and joined them at the kitchen table, frowning as she contemplated what to do next. "I guess the only lead I can pursue is to try and get employment information and references from the law firm handling the Mitchell Trust properties. But that'll have to wait until Monday. And even then, who knows whether they'll be willing to give it to me. The only other thing I can think to do is swing by Jessica's apartment complex and try to catch the upstairs tenants. They're a long shot, at best." She sighed and looked at Tyler. "Any other ideas?"

"Believe me, doll, a lot of detective work is pure grinding along, hoping for a clue or a break in the case. As much as I enjoy working for Crime Tells, I wouldn't want to quit my day job and do it full time."

"But then you have a pretty interesting day job. I think being a police artist would be fun."

Tyler grinned and his eyebrows went up and down. "I get to see a lot of interesting faces—and imagine some outstanding bodies." His look turned mischievous. "Speaking of which, when are you going to let me do some sketches of you? There's a contest I want to enter, and you'd make a great model."

Calista blushed. "Maybe you'd better use Lyric."

He snorted. "Wrong vibes for what I have in mind. But you'd be perfect. Think about it, okay? And in the meantime, I'll put my plate in the sink like a good guest and then head down to the office so I can send Jerick the photo of Jessica."

"You'll call right away if he comes up with anything?"

"You bet." Tyler rose from his chair, moving past Calista and putting his dishes in the sink before returning to stand next to her. Giving her a wink, he leaned down and brushed a kiss across her forehead. "Thanks for breakfast. Does noon work for doing lunch together?"

She laughed. "You're on your own for lunch and dinner today. I'll probably still be in the city."

"Bummer. I sure wish Erin would get back home, or Bulldog would need Cady here for a case."

"You can always drop in on Lyric and Kieran."

"I don't have a death wish, doll. Lyric does a mean mixed drink, but she's not much better in the kitchen than I am. And the thought of having Kieran walk in and find another man in his territory..." Tyler grimaced dramatically. "You know how your brother is..."

Calista snickered. Oh yeah, she knew how her brother was—and she loved watching Lyric drive him crazy. "He trusts you."

"But that doesn't mean he wants to see me in his house, especially when he's probably got plans for his very hot wife."

"Guess you're on your own then."

"I'll head out. Call if you need me."

Dante got up without a word as soon as the front door closed behind Tyler. His dishes joined Tyler's in the sink and then he was standing next to Calista, masculine aggression practically radiating off him. "I'm going to overlook the little display with Tyler," he growled, "because I'm willing to believe at least part of it was him trying to yank my chain. But you will not be posing for any of his sketches unless either Benito's around or I'm around, and believe this, Lista, you *will* have all your clothes on if you do it."

"I'm not going to pose for Tyler," she said, a thrill going through her at Dante's possessiveness—though she wasn't sure whether to thank Tyler for stirring Dante up or be mad at him. She had a case to work on, and despite the way her panties were wet and her cunt was aching, she needed a little bit longer before she could take the Giancottis on again.

"Good. Now go to the bedroom unless you want to risk your neighbors seeing you get a spanking."

Her heart jerked and she stood up. "No."

His face darkened and she knew she'd made a mistake by blurting out her first thought. She tried to undo the damage by saying, "Tyler and I are just friends. You know that!"

"This isn't about Tyler." Dante's hand waved to encompass the folders on the table. "I told you I didn't like the feel of this case and that I'm not going to let you work it alone. And I warned you about holding out on me. Now you can go in the other room, or I can put you over my knee in here. Your choice."

The thought of being punished by Dante was a turn-on. She wasn't going to lie to herself about it. But she didn't want to be punished now, not over this. She was willing to give up a lot of control, she *wanted* to give up control, to have them love and care for her completely. But the case was…somehow outside of that.

Benito had risen to stand behind her, trapping her between him and Dante. She turned to him for support, wrapping her arms around his neck and pressing against him, burying her head against his shoulder. "I didn't do anything wrong. This is *my* case, not his. And besides that, he was sleeping when I decided to call Tyler! I wasn't holding out on him—I didn't even know Tyler had anything until he showed up this morning!"

Benito hugged her to him, brushing a kiss against her hair. "She's got a point, Dante," he said, and Calista shivered as his hand slipped under her dress, stroking over her buttocks. "I think we need to set some ground rules here so everyone's clear on where the lines are."

Dante moved in close enough that she could feel the heat of his body through the thin fabric of her clothing. His hands joined Benito's under her dress, his knuckles moving along the crevice of her ass before his fingers curled around the elastic of her panties and pulled them down, baring her to their touch.

She whimpered as masculine fingers moved through her slit, coating themselves with her juices before swirling over her clit, her swollen, flushed mound, the tight pucker of her anus.

"Okay," Dante growled. "She doesn't go near anyone connected to the Mitchell family without one of us with her. That's the first rule. Second, she keeps us current on where the case is heading and what she's doing."

Benito rubbed his cheek against her hair. "Can you live with those ground rules, Lista?"

She pressed a kiss to his bare chest. "I'll try."

He hugged her, molding his hands to her buttocks and tightening his grip. "Still sore?"

She ached so badly for them that it took all her willpower to say, "Give me until tonight, then we can."

"Okay, sweetheart." His hands slid lower, grasping her panties and starting to pull them up. Dante's fingers rubbed over her clit, making her cry out one more time before he took his hands off her.

Chapter Eleven

They left for San Francisco a little while later, but not before Calista had given each of the three dogs a kiss on the head and a command to "Guard the house". Every time he thought of it, Benito smiled over the image of her doing that. God, she was adorable.

Her house was small, but he'd counted five soft, round dog beds scattered around the place. Hell, the dachshunds probably slept twenty-three hours a day. And yet he could tell she'd be crushed if something happened to one of them. When she loved, she loved with her entire heart.

His own heart quickened and he leaned forward, nuzzling against the side of her face, a pure jolt of happiness bursting through him when he saw her hand entwined with Dante's in the front seat of the Jeep. Christ, he was hooked on her. He knew it had happened fast, but he wanted to tell her he loved her. He wanted to hear her tell him the same thing. And he wanted to know Dante was included.

He cut a look over at his brother. *I like them easy and I like to share them with you. End of story, Benito.* He'd be willing to bet Dante didn't feel that way anymore. The real question was whether or not he'd admit it.

They hit the city just as Dante's cell phone rang. "Shit," he said as soon as he saw the number. Within seconds of taking the call his face was harsh and his voice clipped. "I've got to swing by the station."

"What's wrong?" Calista asked, her voice full of soft concern.

"Nothing for you to worry about." Dante's voice sounded cold and remote.

Benito grimaced when he saw hurt flash across Calista's face. "Trouble with IA?" he guessed, knowing he was right when a muscle twitched in Dante's cheek.

"I'll drop myself off at the station. You and Lista can keep the car," Dante said, not answering Benito's question.

"Keep the car," Benito countered. "Leave us in the Marina District. After we're done checking out Jessica's upstairs neighbors, Calista and I can play tourist. You can call us when you're done and we'll tell you where we are."

Dante left them at Marina Green. "Is he going to be okay?" Calista asked as he drove away. "Do you think this has to do with him being seen at Jessica's apartment building with me yesterday?"

"He'll be fine. Christ, I'll be glad when this mess with the Mitchells is over. Maybe then he'll be ready to turn in the badge." Benito hugged her to him and brushed a kiss against her forehead. "Especially now that we've got you."

Calista's heart felt like it was going to explode in her chest at his words, at the meaning she wanted so desperately to read into them. It felt so right with Benito…it was so easy to believe in forever and happily-ever-after with him.

Crazy. Part of her knew it was crazy to think like that, but then again, she'd seen the magic of love firsthand. She'd grown up hearing about how her father had swept her mother off her feet, marrying her within months of rescuing her from a would-be rapist. Her grandparents were the same, though in their case, her grandmother had "bought" her grandfather at a charity auction to raise money for a new fire engine—an engine her grandfather fought fires from until he retired.

She'd watched Kieran and Lyric and, to a lesser extent, Cady and Kix. She'd seen enough to know what they had was real and lasting and incredibly powerful—though she was realistic enough to know that sometimes their marriages would involve more work than play.

So why should she deny the possibility of love for herself? She'd never felt this way about any of the men she'd dated before, even the ones she'd been intimate with.

Dante and Benito had slept with a lot of women, together, alone, she knew it without being told or coming face-to-face with it by knowing the names and seeing the faces. They were too much like her own brothers and cousins, too much like Cole, Shane and Braden Maguire. They all oozed masculine sensuality, drawing women to them like they'd bathed in some kind of pheromone that made them completely irresistible—even when a woman could tell they were heartbreak in the fast lane.

She wanted to believe it was somehow different with her. That Dante and Benito felt the same way about her as she did about them.

Calista smiled ruefully. Yeah, didn't every woman who tangled with a bad boy think she was the one he'd change for?

Not that she really wanted either Dante or Benito to change—except that she wanted to be the only woman they loved and made love to. There, she'd admitted it to herself. She'd fallen in love with them, not just because of the sex but because loving them felt like coming home to her, like finding a safe place where she could give herself fully, unconditionally. Where her emotional and physical needs meshed perfectly with her partners'. She loved them and she wanted them to love her back. She wanted them to be faithful to her, just as it wasn't even a possibility that she'd sleep with anyone other than them.

"Stop worrying," Benito said, jerking her attention back to him and making her heart skip a few beats at the possibility he'd read what she was thinking in her face. He leaned down, kissing her. "Dante probably got a heads-up on some new PR slant the Mitchells are going to try to make their kids look like angels caught in some huge misunderstanding. Nobody in the department is buying it, and they're not going to leave him out to hang."

For a second her thoughts scrambled between his comment and what he imagined was on her mind versus what actually had been. She kissed him back, then turned her attention to the case.

They walked in the direction of Jessica's apartment complex. When they were a block away, Calista halted and said, "Maybe you should wait here." Benito frowned and she added, "I'll be fine. But if the Mitchells are trying to stir up trouble for Dante by saying he's somehow harassing them, it might be better if no one sees you." She kissed him to take the sting out of her words. "Even with the hair and earring, you're obviously his brother."

She could tell Benito didn't like letting her go off by herself. But he gave in, knowing she had a point, and she got lucky, finding all three of Jessica's upstairs neighbors home.

Two of them didn't bother to open their doors more than a crack, just far enough to tell her they didn't know Jessica and hadn't even spoken to her. The third neighbor, the one whose apartment was directly over Jessica's, had the same look on his time-worn face and probably would have told her the same thing except that when he opened his door, a small red dog dashed out and Calista dropped immediately to her knees, laughing and saying, "Hi there, cutie! I've got three at home just like you!"

"Three?" The door opened wider to reveal an apartment crammed from one end to the other with books.

Calista rose to her feet with the dachshund in her arms. "Three. All a lot older than your," she checked the dog, "girl. Plus mine are all little old men." She blushed, realizing as soon as the words left her mouth that the description fit the man she was talking to.

He took the dog from her arms. "I heard you next door asking about the girl downstairs." He put a finger to his lips before motioning her in with his hand.

Calista hesitated only a minute before stepping into the apartment. The old man peered down the hallway, cocking his head as though listening for something before finally closing his door.

"All clear. No one saw you come in here. Not that either of my neighbors pays much attention. The one next door is too absorbed in his art to see what goes on around him. The one at the end has his boyfriend over. When they're together, you could commit murder in front of them without either of them noticing." He set the dog down, his eyebrows drawing together. "So the cop sent you to see if I ever saw the Mitchell kids or their friends hanging out with the girl downstairs?"

Shock ripped through Calista. He misread the reason and said, "Saw you with him yesterday, so don't bother saying you don't know what I'm talking about."

"You were home?"

"Just getting back when you were talking to Olson. I didn't want him to see me talking to you. Most of the time he's harmless, but he knows who's pulling his strings." The man's smile was sly. "I figured Giancotti would send you back around. Too risky using the phone, not if he wants to stay ahead of the Mitchell family. One son dead and one son looking at prison time—with their rich little friend looking at the same—I wouldn't trust the wheels of justice either if I was Giancotti."

Calista noticed the books then—really noticed them. Mysteries. Espionage stories. True crime dramas. Many of them probably loaded with conspiracy theories. Still, she took her cue from his earlier comment and asked, "So did you ever see the Mitchell kids or their friend with Jessica Winston?"

The old man grinned. "No, but there's a connection. The law firm. Morrisey, Mackall & Dekker. The same one defending the Mitchell kid and his friend. The girl downstairs worked for them. One day a week was all as far as I could tell. Couldn't have been making nearly enough to pay rent for this place. Shared a job with those other pregnant girls. One of them worked Tuesdays, the other worked on Wednesday. Jessica was the Friday girl. Might have been a couple of others working Mondays and Thursdays, but they didn't come around. The others didn't come around either until the last couple of months."

His eyes twinkled with excitement. "You know about the babies, right? All of them going up for adoption."

Calista nodded. "Did any of them know who was adopting their child?"

"Not as far as I could tell. Sometimes they'd sit around in the backyard, but they didn't talk much about the babies except to complain about being pregnant. Mostly they gushed over clothing and what they were going to do when they were thin and had plenty of money to spend. Sometimes they complained about the lawyers in their office. I could only take so much before I closed the window." He shrugged. "Overall, not a very interesting bunch."

"Even Jessica?"

"They were all pretty much interchangeable as far as I could tell. Probably hadn't read an entire book between them since they left school." His gaze sharpened on Calista. "What about you? Are you a reader?"

"Yes. Mysteries, science fiction, romance, children's books, lots and lots of children's books." She laughed, startled and a little flustered at having revealed so much about herself.

There was no hiding the intelligence behind his eyes. "You're no private investigator, or if you are, you haven't been one for very long." He nodded as if he approved of his own conclusion. "Giancotti is smart, sending someone like you out to ask questions and try and get a lock on the case. You're about as threatening as a kindergarten teacher who is big on cookies and milk and wouldn't know one end of a paddle from the other." He chuckled. "Guess that dates me. It's been a long time since teachers could discipline their students."

Calista was torn between crying and laughing at having been made for a kindergarten teacher. She tried to get the conversation back to Jessica by asking, "Anything else you can tell me about her? Any other friends come by? Anything odd happen?"

The old man shook his head. "Nope. Kept pretty quiet overall. Gone a lot of the time. Early on, when she first moved in, there was a guy who came around a couple of times. Dressed nicely. Drove a fancy sports car. Haven't seen him in a couple of years. Haven't seen any other guys since him. If she had friends, she didn't bring them home."

Calista wasn't surprised. She still couldn't get a fix on exactly who Jessica was, other than secretive and cautious.

"If you think of anything else, will you call me?" she asked, realizing she didn't even know the man's name.

He nodded slowly. "There's a pay phone down the street. But I won't talk. If I call at all, I'll just say I was looking for Mr. Smith but I think I have the wrong number. That'll be your signal to come around again."

Calista nodded solemnly before thanking him for his help and leaving the apartment.

"You were gone a long time," Benito said, pulling her into his arms when she got back to where she'd left him. "Learn anything?"

She'd known he was going to ask, still she hesitated, not wanting to lie but feeling like she needed to talk to Lyric or Tyler before revealing what Jessica's neighbor had said to either Benito or Dante. In an effort to divert his attention she asked, "Do I look like a kindergarten teacher?"

Benito laughed. "Yeah. You do. Is that what one of the neighbors said?"

"Yes. He had a dachshund just like my guys, only younger and female. He said I made him think of a kindergarten teacher who's big on cookies and milk and wouldn't know one end of a paddle from the other."

Benito laughed again before brushing a kiss across her mouth. "Is that so terrible?"

"No one would accuse Lyric of being a teacher," she grumbled. "Or Cady or Erin."

"No," Benito agreed. "I don't know Erin or Cady, but you're definitely not like your sister-in-law." He kissed her again. "But that's not a terrible thing as far as I'm concerned. I like everything about you, Lista, and I wouldn't change a thing."

His voice rang with such sincerity that she felt guilty about not volunteering *everything* Jessica's neighbor had said. She would, eventually, but she needed some time to think about it, some time to understand better why her case seemed to run into the Mitchell family at every turn.

She shivered, remembering the ground rules she'd agreed to earlier—to keep them current on where the case was heading and what she was doing, *and* not to go near anyone connected to the Mitchell family without either Benito or Dante going with her. She knew she was going to have to visit Morrisey, Mackall & Dekker—but she'd tell them after she went. It wasn't like either one of them *could* go with her.

"You told Dante we were going to play tourist when we were done here," she said, wanting to keep Benito from asking any more questions. "Let's go to Golden Gate Park. I've only been there once, on a field trip when I was a kid."

They went, joining a throng of city dwellers and tourists, spending time seeing the sights until the need to stay in one place and concentrate on each other got to be too much to ignore. Then they found a spot and settled on the grass, sitting at first, talking and kissing until they ended up stretched out side by side.

Calista looked at Benito from under lowered eyelashes and used a hand on his chest to push him onto his back. He laughed, the glint in his eyes telling her he enjoyed her small show of aggression.

She draped her leg over his and rose up on an elbow so she could fully appreciate how gorgeous he was. She'd always gone for dark-haired men, but none of them could hold a candle to Benito and Dante.

Unable to keep from touching him, she trailed her finger down his straight, aristocratic nose before tracing very kissable lips and then moving to spread his long hair out on either side of him.

The diamond in his ear sparkled and her fingers moved to toy with it. He gasped, a small sound of arousal that had her body tightening. "Every time I see this, I want to put my mouth on it," she said, teasing him with light touches to his earlobe before gently exploring the shell of his ear.

His laugh was husky and aroused. "I wouldn't recommend doing that right now, or we'll end up being hauled down to the police station. I don't think Dante would like having to bail us out."

Calista's eyes moved to the front of his jeans, to the prominent bulge. "Unbutton your shirt," she said, whispering the order, once again seeing his amusement, the quick smile that told her he was *allowing* her to tell him what to do.

His hands moved slowly down the light blue shirt, unbuttoning it but not opening it. Calista leaned over him and peeled it back, exposing the naturally browned tone of his skin, the small, tight male nipples.

She couldn't resist exploring them with her fingers, thrilling at the way his abdomen tightened and the bulge in his pants grew, at the way his breathing became more rapid. "Lista," he warned.

"I love touching you." She smoothed her hand down the center of his chest, over his stomach, just barely brushing against the waistband of his jeans.

He groaned, grabbing her fingers and holding them pressed against his hot flesh. "I've only got so much control around you," he said, touching her core with his admission. "Let's go to Dante's apartment."

She nodded, thrilled at how quickly he rose to his feet and pulled her up, at how quickly he hustled her to his brother's apartment.

They were barely inside when he began stripping out of his clothing, stopping only to kiss her and help her out of hers.

And then they were on the bed, rolling around, desperate for the feel of skin on skin, touching, kissing, hungry for each other. "God, Lista, I love touching you too," he said, reversing the positions they'd been in at the park, his face inches from hers, his leg thrown over hers so that his cock pressed against her thigh.

She wound her arms around his neck, lifting herself and closing the distance between their lips. "Make love to me," she whispered.

It was all he could do to resist her, to keep from shifting a few inches and thrusting into her welcoming heat. God, he wanted to make love to her, but he also wanted to wait for Dante. Last night had been heaven and hell—to be in the same bed with her and not be able to do more than kiss and pet—Christ, he needed her. They both needed her.

With a groan, he pulled away and repositioned them so that as he worked his way down her body, kissing her, hungrily sucking at her lips, her neck, she could do the same to him. She whimpered and writhed underneath him, and when he reached her nipples and felt her hot, wet, mouth latch on to his own, he nearly came on the sheets.

Her tongue and teeth had him crying out, bucking and panting and wondering if he'd last long enough to reach the sweet destination of her cunt. To lick and suckle her there as she took his cock in her mouth.

"Lista," he cried out, panting, levering himself away from her long enough to get his control back. She followed, crying out at the loss of him, latching onto one nipple then kissing a path to the other. "God, Lista, I'm not going to last."

"I don't care."

He groaned, settling back on her, burying his face in her breasts before forcing himself to move lower, to explore her delicate bellybutton, the flat little belly, and then the paradise of her bare cunt with its swollen lips and erect clit.

Benito was lost at the first taste of her. At the way she opened herself wider, offering him everything even as she worshipped his cock with her mouth. Driving him higher with each stroke of her tongue, each pull of her lips.

He gave up any semblance of control then. His body wanting only to please and be pleased. To completely love and be loved by the woman underneath him.

Afterward they showered together, their touches softer, less desperate, but no less loving. And then they climbed back into bed and snuggled until finally drifting into a nap.

* * * * *

Fuck. He should have known he'd find them like this. Hell, maybe he had known. Maybe this was the real reason he'd come back to his apartment rather than phoning Benito and tracking them down. He'd told himself he needed time to decompress, to think about the latest bullshit the Mitchells and their lawyer were laying down—because there was no doubt in his mind that they were behind it. Even Donner from Internal Affairs didn't really buy into the pissant junkie suddenly coming forward with a story about seeing Dante meeting more than once with the dealer John Mitchell had killed.

Goddamn, he was sick of this.

Dante stripped out of his clothes and slid under the covers, his heart and gut twisting with wild, unfamiliar emotion when Calista made a little sound and turned, snuggling up to him, accepting him, welcoming him even in her sleep. Christ, he needed this. Needed to be close to them both right now when it felt like his life was going to shit.

As if sensing his distress, she pressed closer, wedging her thigh between his legs and putting her arm over his side, hugging him to her. He buried his face in her hair, breathing deeply, loving the way she smelled.

Last night had been the first time he'd ever slept with a woman all night and done nothing but pet and talk to her. And even that had been incredible with Calista.

Hell, before she'd come along, he'd barely cared enough to get a first name from the women he slept with. But with her, the more he knew, the more he wanted to know.

Have you ever wondered what it would be like with a woman we actually cared about? One who belonged just to us? One who wanted more from us than a good time and a great fuck story to tell her friends? A woman we could have together or separately? One who saw us as individuals who came as a package deal? One who was waiting for us at the end of the day?

Benito's words rolled through Dante and lodged deep in his soul. Christ, he'd never wondered, never even been tempted to, but now she was here, wrenching open old wounds and healing them with her caring, making it impossible to imagine not having her, not having this with her.

Calista woke and brushed a kiss against his chest, whispering, "What's wrong?" and his heart flooded with something so fragile he didn't want to look too hard for fear it would escape. Her concern just about undid him. Besides Benito, no one in his life had ever loved him.

He tightened his hold on her, wanting to soak everything she offered right through his skin. Fuck, she'd found a way into his heart and he didn't think he'd ever get her out of it. Maybe Benito was right, maybe when this mess with the Mitchell kid and his friend was over he'd give up the badge and take over part of Giancotti Security. Between the cop hours and the commute, he'd never get to be with them enough otherwise.

Benito stirred and opened his eyes. "You okay?"

"Yeah." It came out gruff, but he didn't want to talk right now. He needed something else, desperately. Without a word he pulled the sheet down, his eyes going instantly to Benito's cock and seeing it was ready—full and flushed and hard—a mirror image of his own. His gaze shifted, their eyes locked and he knew Benito could see what he needed, understood without words exactly how much he needed it—and wanted the same thing.

Benito shifted to his back, kicking the covers the rest of the way off as Dante smoothed his hand over Calista's ass before saying, "Get on Benito, Lista. Put his cock in you."

Her breath gave a little hitch and she pulled back far enough so she could look at him from underneath her eyelashes. Christ, he loved how she did that, acknowledging with such a simple gesture how much she liked having him dominate her in bed. How willing she was to give him what he needed.

Without a word she did as he'd commanded, straddling Benito, her delicate, feminine hand taking his brother's cock and guiding it to her entrance before she lowered her body onto it, her nipples becoming tight buds as Dante watched. She whimpered softly, a sound that had his own penis pulsing with anticipation, but when she would have started riding Benito, Dante's hand burned her ass with a sharp slap. "I didn't tell you to do that. Lie down on him, Lista, and don't move. If I see you fucking yourself on his cock, I'm going to spank you again."

He watched intently as she stretched out on Benito, felt a jolt of incredible sexual heat when she was unable to keep herself from grinding against his brother's groin. He spanked her again, intensely aroused by her small cry of pained pleasure, by the sight of Benito's hands moving over her reddened ass cheeks, ready to spread them so Dante could tunnel into her nearly virgin back entrance.

Dante could see her shaking against Benito, knowing what was coming, fearing it even as she anticipated it. Christ. He wanted to play with her longer, to drive up the pleasure for all of them, but he didn't think he could hold off. He needed this too badly. Needed to be inside her. Needed to feel Benito inside her. He needed to be close to them both.

Calista bit down on her bottom lip to keep from whimpering as Benito's hands moved over her buttocks. Her heart was racing, the blood thundering through her body and pulsing into her clit in sharp bursts. She couldn't stop herself from shivering, from rubbing her cheek against Benito's hot skin.

"You want this, don't you, Lista?" he whispered into her hair.

"Yes."

"You know we'll take care of you, we'll make it good for you?"

She pressed a kiss against his chest, her heart swelling with love. They made her feel so safe, so adored. "Yes."

Benito tightened his hold on her momentarily. God he loved her. He needed her. She was his refuge, his paradise. His eyes met Dante's and he read the same thoughts, the same need in his brother's face.

Dante retrieved the lubricant from the nightstand and moved over them, his fingers circling and dipping into her back entrance, preparing her as her whimpers made him reach for his own cock for fear of coming from the sounds she was making and the sight of Benito's cock lodged inside her.

Always before it had been about the twin-bond, about sharing something intense with his brother. It had been about the two of them—and the woman sandwiched between them hadn't been important.

Not anymore. Not with Calista.

He should be scared at how she'd changed the need, made it impossible to imagine sharing this with anyone else other than her—but he couldn't work up enough fear to keep a barrier around his soul or his heart.

With a groan he covered her body, kissing her neck and shoulders as he slowly worked himself in. "That's it, baby," he whispered, feeling the way she was trying to relax, to make it easier for him to get inside her tight little hole. And then he was all the way in, separated from Benito by a thin barrier—both of them held tightly in her welcoming heat.

For a long moment Dante savored the heaven of her, savored the closeness, not moving until his gaze met Benito's in a silent communication that had taken on a deeper meaning with Calista held between them. Then without words, they began thrusting and counter thrusting, soaking up her cries of pleasure as they loved her together, as they found comfort in each other and with her.

Chapter Twelve

Sunday passed in a blur of sex and conversation, movies and jokes and even a Tinkertoys versus Legos challenge that ended in a draw and left Calista laughing at the strange machines and buildings Dante and Benito had created from the toys she'd bought for her classroom.

They managed to avoid talking about her case or about what had forced Dante to the police station on Saturday, though the first was easier to do than the second, since the newspapers screamed with information—a supposed leak revealing a witness had come forward claiming Dante and the dead drug dealer had been seen together numerous times, along with a sly reminder that Dante was not on the vice squad.

Monday came too soon, and yet not soon enough.

"Dinner at our place tonight?" Benito said as they stood near her front door.

"I can't. I'm going to Echoes with Lyric and my cousin Sierra tonight."

His frown was immediate. "That place is a meat market!"

She brushed a kiss across his lips. "Yes it is. And Monday is ladies night, so we get in free."

"Lista…"

She laughed at the mix of emotions crossing his face—then took pity on him. "Don't worry. Nothing I see at Echoes will come anywhere close to what I've seen and had in my own bed this weekend. We're only going there because it's country music night. They give line-dance lessons and we want to know how for when we visit Cady and Kix in Texas."

"Is your brother going to be there?"

"Probably not. Kieran doesn't do country—though once he starts thinking about Lyric dancing with other men, even in a line…" She wrinkled her nose. "He's kind of a caveman. But I think Lyric said he's working on a case and doing stakeouts at night."

Benito rubbed his nose along hers. "So you won't mind if Dante and I show up?"

She hesitated for only a second before saying. "No."

"You're sure?"

She knew what he was really asking. Having Tyler know she was sleeping with both Benito and Dante was one thing, but was she really prepared for Lyric and her cousin to see the three of them together? To speculate on what was going on between them? Not that they'd be obvious—but…it would be obvious they were close.

"It's okay. What time will you get back from LA?"

"Don't know, but early enough to meet you at Echoes." He sighed and checked his watch. "You've got my cell number and Dante's, call if you need us, okay?"

Her cunt clenched and her arms tightened around him. She'd had more sex in a single weekend with them than she'd *ever* had—even if she counted every single encounter before meeting them and condensed them into the same amount of time.

She couldn't stop herself from laughing and saying, "I think you guys have turned me into a sex maniac. Dante's only been gone a couple of hours and you're not even through my front door yet, but I already *need* you."

Benito grinned, hugging her tight, kissing her as one hand roamed down her back and across her buttocks. "I'm glad to hear that, sweetheart, because I can pretty much guarantee I'm going to be walking around with a hard-on and thinking about you all day. You sure you have to go with Lyric and Sierra tonight?"

"Positive."

"I'll see you at Echoes then." He pressed another quick kiss to her lips. "I better get going."

"Me, too." He frowned and she mentally grimaced, rushing to head off any questions about what she had planned for the day by saying, "I'm heading to Crime Tells. I need to bring Bulldog up to speed on the case, plus I want to get my notes typed into the computer at the office."

He visibly relaxed and she felt a little guilty for misdirecting him, for not telling him everything she had planned. But she'd had over a day to think about it, and she still couldn't see any good coming out of telling them she intended to visit Morrisey, Mackall & Dekker. She'd tell them after she'd done it. That would be soon enough.

* * * * *

Cruz Damascus was the only one in the office when she got to Crime Tells. He looked up from the computer and smiled. "Hey, Teach. Word travels. Heard you got the job and got a first case."

Calista moved over and leaned against the desk he shared with Cole Maguire and Erin. She didn't know him well, and what she did know came mostly through Lyric.

He'd been a boxer once, and he still looked the part. But somehow he'd ended up in one of Cole's poker clinics and Cole had been so impressed he'd talked Cruz into interviewing with Bulldog.

"What are you working on?" she asked.

He laughed and shifted the monitor so she could see the screen. Poker. She should have known. Cruz smiled, white teeth against beautiful mahogany skin. "Just continuing my education, Teach. Got a deck of cards in the desk drawer if you want to practice."

Calista wrinkled her nose. "No, I don't think I want to start the day off losing. Is Bulldog in?"

"Just missed him. He's heading north to one of the Indian casinos for a consult." His eyes took in Calista's outfit. "What about you? You look like you're heading to an interview. Not giving up the PI gig already, are you?"

"I've got to visit some lawyers in San Francisco."

"Want some company?"

Her first instinct was to say yes. Her second was to wonder if she should say no. So far she hadn't gone anywhere by herself... She nibbled on her bottom lip. Of course, it wasn't like she was *used* to being alone when she worked—from the moment she got to school in the morning until the moment she drove out of the parking lot, she was interacting with other people.

As if sensing her inner battle, Cruz settled it for her by standing up. "We can take your car, hit the lawyers first, then there's a gym I want to stop by. I think it's something you'd be interested in."

She gave in, waiting long enough for him to close his poker program before leaving Crime Tells.

The lawyers' office was downtown in a building that oozed prestige and money. "Morrisey, Mackall & Dekker," Cruz said as they moved into the elevator and hit the button. "The name's sounding familiar, but I can't place it."

"They've been in the news lately, representing Paul Mitchell."

Cruz gave a soft whistle. "Little bird told me you were seen with the cop involved in that."

"Lyric?"

He laughed. "Gotta keep my sources confidential. Man that talks stops getting talked to."

She laughed. "What about being a team player and all that?"

He flashed her a smile. "Still working my way around that idea, Teach. In the ring it's one man standing on his own against another man."

Calista worried on her bottom lip, curious about why he'd given up boxing but hesitant to pry and inadvertently cause him pain. He caught the look and the humor left his face. "You got the same look in your eye my third-grade teacher used to give me when I'd piss myself at the end of the day because it was time to go home. I killed a man. Put him down in the third round. Doing it made me realize I didn't need to keep punching at my past anymore, that I didn't need to fight in a ring to prove myself."

She reached over and curled her hand around his biceps, giving him a squeeze. "Thanks for telling me."

The laughter returned to his face and he covered her hand with his. "Teach, enjoy your summer break. But come fall, go back to your classroom. You're not near tough enough for this job, and there are a bunch of kids who need you more."

She gave him a mock scowl before pulling her hand away from his arm just as the elevator glided to a stop.

Morrisey, Mackall & Dekker smelled like money — the kind that said, if you've got it, then we can get you off, no matter what crime you've committed.

"I'll wait for you here," Cruz said, taking a seat on a plush sofa and picking up a neatly folded *Wall Street Journal*.

Calista moved to the reception desk and was immediately ushered down the hall to an office with a window and an austere, gray-suited woman behind a desk meant to convey a huge discrepancy between whoever was sitting in front of it and her. "You're here about Jessica Winston? May I see some identification, please?" Her clipped voice said she was well used to intimidating people.

Calista pulled out a business card and took the offensive. "My official cards haven't arrived, but please feel free to call Bulldog, he can verify my employment."

The woman studied the card for a second before placing it on her desk and picking up an expensive pen. "C.a.l.l.i.s.t.a."

"One l."

"Burke, with an 'e' on the end?"

"Yes." Calista surreptitiously studied the desk for a name. Irene Lee.

"Personnel records are confidential," Irene told her, setting the pen aside.

"Jessica's family has hired us to put together a portrait of what her life in San Francisco was like," Calista said, hedging the truth as she studied Irene's expression and concluded that if she got anything from this woman, it would be because the law firm thought it was in *their* best interests.

So what did she really want from this visit? Confirmation that Jessica put the baby up for adoption? The name of the adoption agency or the lawyer handling it? No, she wanted a chance to talk to co-workers because then she'd get a lot more information.

Calista adopted the approach she used when she had to conference with parents of difficult children — confidence with a "we're here to help each other" attitude. "I'm afraid that, so far, the portrait of Jessica is a disappointing one. Apparently she first made money by selling her eggs to a clinic run by Dr. Lassiter. Then, as you know, she became a surrogate mother and placed her child up for adoption. I understand several other girls were in a similar situation and they all shared a job here, with Jessica working on Fridays." Calista mentally crossed her fingers and prayed Jessica's upstairs neighbor knew what he was talking about.

"Quite frankly, I'd prefer to have something more positive to tell her parents. They're not interested in how much she made or anything like that. Mainly I'd like to talk to some of her co-workers so I can give the Winstons a more positive overall view of their daughter as they look for closure."

Irene Lee's face didn't give away a single thought. Nor did any part of her body. It remained completely unmoving as a heavy silence settled around them.

Calista smiled to herself and made no effort to either break the stare or fill the void with nervous conversation. Outwaiting kindergarteners who didn't want to do an assignment had left her well prepared for this kind of warfare.

It was Irene Lee who broke first, not completely dismissing Calista's request but not giving her what she wanted either. "I'm afraid the girls who shared Jessica's position are no longer with the firm. I would need to speak with one of the partners before releasing their names to you. Unfortunately, none of them is currently available."

"What about Jessica's other co-workers? A supervisor perhaps?"

Irene's mouth formed a grim line. "Once again, I would need to clear the matter with one of the partners." She glanced briefly at the Crime Tells card before standing, forcing Calista to do the same. "I know how to get in touch with you, Ms. Burke. I'll contact you if we can help you in this matter."

Calista nodded, fairly certain she wouldn't hear from them. The certainty grew when she visited the law firm dealing with the Mitchell rental properties and was told they couldn't locate Jessica's application.

"That's the way it goes," Cruz said as he maneuvered out of the parking garage where they'd left her car. "You stir the shit, see if anything sticks. Throw out some feelers and reel in what you can. Then start all over again."

Calista sighed. She felt like she was running out of places to start.

They stopped at a little hole-in-the-wall Mexican restaurant in a rough area of town and ate before going to the gym. Calista looked around, feeling way out of her element—and worried briefly whether or not her car was going to be okay.

Cruz laughed and put his arm around her shoulder, hugging her to him in a gesture that looked more intimate than it felt. "Got a truce working here right now. You're with me. The car is with me. You'll both be fine." He opened the door of a run-down building with paper grocery bags and yellowed newspapers taped to the windows so no one could see in—or out.

Calista paused in the doorway. The smell was almost overwhelming—like being trapped in a small classroom on a hot day with three dozen sweaty boys.

Cruz laughed again and took an exaggerated breath. "Got a lot of memories rolled into the smell of a gym. Same as you probably have when you get a whiff of crayons and paste."

She couldn't help herself. Calista smiled and snaked an arm around his waist, giving him a quick, affectionate hug.

"Amigo!" A beefy guy yelled from where he was standing next to a punching bag. "This your woman? *Muy bonita!* You're lucky, amigo. Come and watch Esteban! Give him some pointers."

Cruz released Calista and pointed her in another direction, calling her attention to a group of children gathered around a table. She couldn't resist, and almost as soon as she'd joined them, she was hooked—drawn into helping them with their math worksheets after one wiry eight-year-old told her, "My man Hector said he wasn't teaching nobody how to use their fists if they wasn't also learning how to use their heads."

A couple of hours later, as they were leaving the gym, Calista teased, "Is that why you bought me lunch? You knew I was going to end up working?"

"Bought us both lunch. I put my time in too." He balled up his fists and made a few jabs into the air.

She reached over and squeezed his biceps. "Thanks for bringing me here."

A car came around the corner. There was a bang and an explosion of glass, but before Calista could react, Cruz had plowed into her, knocking her to the sidewalk and rolling her against the car, his front to her back.

More gunshots fired, hitting the gym window. From inside the building, male voices yelled to get down and stay away from the window, but the car with the gunman was already disappearing down the street even as Cruz was opening his cell phone. Calista lay there, heart thundering in her ears, scared, until thoughts of the children brought her to her feet.

They were okay. Thank God. Animated. Scared—maybe—but not showing it, not in front of these muscled fighters they wanted to impress with their toughness.

"Cruz okay?" the man who'd first greeted them asked.

"Yes." She glanced down and noticed her hands were shaking. But before she could hide them by shoving them into her pockets, the man yelled, "Esteban! Get the lady a Coke-a-cola."

The lanky kid who'd been at the punching bag earlier said, "Sure, Hector," and moved toward a door leading to an office.

"I'm okay," Calista said as sirens sounded in the distance.

Hector looked her over and yelled again, "Esteban! Bring out the first-aid kit, too!" He winked at Calista. "Wouldn't usually bother with cuts and scrapes like you've got, but I don't want the boys to get the idea it's okay for a pretty woman to walk around bleeding."

Calista looked down, suddenly aware of the burning along her calf. She grimaced in anticipation of Dante and Benito's reaction. "Cruz said this was a safe place."

Hector shrugged. "Most of the time it is. But there's always going to be those who don't want to see anybody else make something of themselves."

Chapter Thirteen

Dante tightened his hold on the steering wheel. Son of a bitch. His heart still felt like it was going to roar right out of his chest. Christ. What the hell had she been doing there? And why hadn't she told him she was coming to the city today?

Fuck. She was going to feel his hand across her ass this time even if he had to break Benito's arms to get her out of them.

Goddammit, it had been a day straight from hell. First the junkie who'd claimed there was a connection between Dante and the dealer the Mitchell kid killed got popped in a drive-by shooting in Hunter's Point. Then witnesses swore the shooter was in a black Wrangler just like Dante's.

Why didn't the Mitchells have them give my fucking license plate number while they were at it? he'd raged, glad his car was down in police parking and Benito was out of town. Christ! The DA must have something on the Mitchell kid and his friend for the family to be taking these kinds of risks. A dead junkie meant a witness who couldn't change what was in the police report or say he was paid to say it.

What was going on? The character smear in the papers was one thing, but this?

Yeah. He wasn't the only one asking that question.

"You stir up some shit we don't know about?" his captain had asked. Internal Affairs had asked the same.

Dante had ended up at the station all day—going over facts, slogging through paperwork, sitting in meetings and throwing around ideas, waiting for reports from Hunter's Point to trickle in while he was tied to the police station in an informal protective custody so it'd be impossible to connect him to the drive-by.

And he'd lingered afterward—not exactly in a hurry to get to Echoes and find himself in a line-dance lesson. Now he couldn't get there fast enough.

Son of a bitch. He'd just about lost it when the captain had dropped his bomb. Walking into the bullpen with a frown that had his eyebrows pulled together into one long bushy line. "Giancotti, what's the name of that woman you were with on Friday, at the Mitchell rental over in the Marina District?"

"Calista Burke."

The captain skimmed the paper in his hand, his eyebrows pressing against each other so hard they started to dip. "She's a PI for Bulldog Montgomery's outfit? Isn't Burke the name of the vice cop who's married to Bulldog's granddaughter?"

"Yeah."

"You might want to stay away from her for a while, Giancotti. She was standing in front of Hector's Gym when someone sprayed the place with bullets earlier this afternoon."

Dante was out of his seat and reaching for his jacket, ready to turn in his badge on the spot if they tried to keep him at the station a second longer. They weren't that foolish.

His cell phone rang. "Are you with her?" he demanded, seeing Benito's number and answering.

"No. Just got off the plane, checked my messages and found yours."

"Christ! Have you talked to her?"

"A couple of hours ago."

"What the fuck was she doing in San Francisco? And why the hell was she in that part of town?"

"Back up, bro. What's going on?"

"She didn't tell you?"

"Tell me what? When I talked to her, she and Lyric were at her cousin's house, trying to decide how country they wanted to dress. They're probably at Echoes now, which is where I'm heading as soon as I get home, take a quick shower and change."

"Son of a bitch. She's going to feel my hand on her backside tonight."

There was a long sigh on the other end of the line. "You going to keep ranting and make me guess what's got you so wound up, or are you going to just tell me so I don't end up in the middle again if she doesn't think she deserves to be punished?"

Dante told him and Benito said, "I won't get between you and her."

* * * * *

"How's the leg?" Lyric asked as they plopped down in their seats for a breather when the last line-dance lesson of the night ended.

"Not bad. I think the dancing is actually helping, keeping everything loosened up."

Sierra grimaced. "Expect to see Kieran at your doorstep as soon as some cop in San Francisco makes the connection and calls him."

Lyric grinned. "And knowing him, after he tries to talk Calista into going back to teaching, he'll probably decide that my encouraging her to work for Bulldog in the first place is a punishable offense."

All three women snickered and Lyric raised her beer bottle in the air. "To dominant men, you gotta love 'em. Speaking of which," Lyric said after she'd taken a swallow of beer, "here comes one with a hard-on for Calista. And from the look of him, he's either not very happy to find her here, or he heard about the drive-by."

Calista turned and saw Dante bearing down on her. Her cunt tightened in reaction to the dark, completely controlled expression on his face.

"Let's go," he said, not even bothering to acknowledge Sierra or Lyric as he wrapped his hand around Calista's arm and tried to haul her to her feet.

"I'm not ready to leave yet," she said, using her legs around the chair to keep him from dislodging her from her seat.

A muscle twitched in his cheek. "I'm not playing, Lista. I want to talk to you."

"Then talk to me on the dance floor. Or sit down here and talk." A jolt of heat seared her belly at her own boldness in defying him.

He took a seat, leaning forward so only she could hear him. "Baby, you're just making it worse for yourself. The longer you try and avoid your punishment, the hotter your little ass is going to get when I finally get you home and put you over my knee."

Moisture flooded her panties and her clit throbbed at his threat. "I didn't do anything wrong."

"You went to the city without telling either Benito or me you were doing it. You went into a very dangerous area where you had no business going. And you did it after agreeing to keep us informed." His fingers speared through her hair and tightened just painfully enough to send a small thrill of erotic fear through her. "Don't think Benito's going to interfere this time, Lista. Don't think he's going to keep you from getting a spanking. Now let's go."

Calista shivered, tempted to stand and let him take her home. To let him punish her and then make love to her.

She resisted the temptation, realizing that while she was willing to surrender everything when they were in the bedroom, she didn't want to become the type of woman who lost her independence out in public, who dropped her own plans because the man, or men, in her life ordered her to. She and Lyric and Sierra had been looking forward to tonight and she didn't want to leave just because Dante had shown up.

"No," she told him again. "I want to stay a little while longer." Then, taking a leaf from Lyric's book, she decided to go for the gusto, daring to stir him up further—and praying Benito didn't take too long to get here. "But if you want to go home and wait for me…"

The thunderclouds in his face and the promise of complete domination in his eyes stopped her, and she remembered too late his previous warnings. *You don't want to disobey me, Lista. You don't want to push too many of my buttons.*

She escaped to the dance floor with Lyric and Sierra and stayed there until Benito arrived, joining them in a line-dance before they all returned to the table, finishing their drinks and ordering fresh ones.

"So what were you doing at Hector's Gym?" Benito asked, his fingers entwined with Calista's, his voice casual though she could feel the tension in his body.

Heat rushed to her face at the very speculative looks Sierra and Lyric were giving her. Damn. She should have told them when they were at Sierra's house. It had been on the tip of her tongue…well, close. She'd tried a time or two to come up with a good opening, something other than, "Dante and Benito Giancotti might show up, and yes, I'm sleeping with them both."

Now she could tell it was only a matter of time before Lyric and Sierra dragged her to the ladies' room so they could force a "true confession" out of her. Calista grimaced and look a long swallow of her mixed drink. And after the confession with Lyric and Sierra, she still had to face Benito and Dante. At some point she'd have to admit she'd been to the law offices of Morrisey, Mackall & Dekker. That actually worried her a lot more than telling them about Hector's Gym.

Benito squeezed her hand, silently reminding her he'd asked a question. She squeezed back. "Cruz Damascus took me to the gym. He mentors there and he thought I'd find it interesting." At their immediate frowns, she added, "Cruz works for Bulldog."

"So you went to San Francisco just to visit a gym?" Benito asked.

She knew she looked guilty when she saw his eyes harden into almost mirror images of Dante's. Her stomach flipped over. It had never occurred to her that he might punish her too.

"I was following up on a lead," she said. "But it didn't go anywhere."

A muscle jerked in Dante's cheek. Lyric stepped in, diverting the conversation away from Calista by mentioning the shooting in Hunter's Point.

"Christ, what's got the Mitchells so scared?" Benito asked, echoing the question that had been floating around the police station since the junkie was killed. "It can't be a coincidence he got popped."

"Smart way of doing it, though," Lyric said. "You've got to give them credit. No way to prove the junkie wasn't just in the wrong place at the wrong time. And they left themselves plenty of wiggle room in case Dante had an alibi. There are a lot of Jeep Wranglers around, enough so the vehicle could be his — or not."

Sierra frowned. "If it was supposed to look like the junkie-turned-informant was in the wrong place at the wrong time, then what about the shooting at Hector's Gym? How do we know that wasn't a message for Dante?"

Calista felt a rush of dizziness.

At first she attributed it to the shock of Sierra's wild speculation that she'd been the intended target at Hector's Gym. But the dizziness persisted, and with it came a vague sense of nausea. She stood, not liking how awkward her limbs felt. She hadn't drunk that much, had she? Two drinks, and the first one had been spread out as they went back and forth from the dance floor. She tried to focus on her latest drink. There was only a little bit left. Maybe she'd drunk it too fast. But she'd eaten, right? She was having a little trouble remembering if they'd had dinner before coming to Echoes and that scared her.

"I'll be back," she said, aiming in the direction of the restrooms.

Lyric and Sierra were out of their chairs in a shot, though neither of them said anything until they'd gotten to the ladies' room. "You okay?" Sierra asked. "You don't look good, Callie."

Calista tried to frown at her cousin for using that particular nickname, but she couldn't get her face to work correctly. "I feel weird," she whispered. "Really, really strange."

Lyric studied her closer. "She only had two drinks, right?"

"Yes," Sierra said.

"Two drinks shouldn't do this to her." Lyric moved closer, getting right in Calista's face before saying, "Shit. Go get one of the guys…try and make it Benito…I'm going to see if I can get her to throw up."

Calista wanted to protest. They were talking about her like she wasn't there! She hated to see parents and teachers do that. She'd send a note home, along with the handout on teaching respect by mirroring it for children. And maybe she should send the one on how self-esteem… The door opened, letting in a blast of music and jarring her out of her thoughts. Why was she thinking about school? She wasn't a teacher any more. Tears formed.

Lyric lightly tapped her cheek and she blinked. "You need to try and throw up," she said, guiding Calista into a toilet stall. "I think someone put something in your drink." Then in a firmer voice, "Stick your finger down your throat if you have to, Calista. Hurry up and do it before Dante or Benito barges in here."

Dante reached them first. One look at Sierra's face and his cop instincts took over. He was out of his chair and striding to the ladies' restroom before Calista's cousin got the first word out.

"What's wrong with her?" he asked, pushing through the bathroom door and sending a couple of primping women into drunken squeals.

Lyric tossed the wet paper towel she'd been using on Calista's face into the trashcan and moved out of Dante's way before he knocked her out of it. "I'd guess a date-rape drug by the way she's acting."

Dante scooped a nearly unconscious Calista into his arms and carried her out of the bathroom and out of the club. They'd just about gotten to Benito's truck when a police car pulled in with its lights flashing, stopping behind the pickup and blocking it in. A young cop in a uniform got out, hand on the butt of his service revolver.

Benito was the first to speak. "We've got an emergency here. We need to get her to the hospital. Follow us there if you need to."

The cop took a moment to assess the situation, then backed off, climbing into his car and getting out of the way, no doubt calling in Benito's plate number as he did.

Lyric grimaced and called Kieran. He made it to the hospital just as they did and recognized the cop who'd come in with them. "Thanks for the escort, Frazier."

The cop seemed momentarily confused and then extremely uncomfortable when he saw the brief hug between Lyric and Kieran. "Uh, Kieran, can we talk a minute?"

Kieran shot the uniformed cop a quick glance, pausing long enough for Calista, Dante and Benito to disappear down a hallway lined with curtained exam rooms. Frustrated, angry, worried about seeing his baby sister drugged and unconscious, Kieran directed a blistering question at Lyric. "What the fuck's she doing with them both? I told him to stay away from her!"

The officer cleared his throat. "Uh, Kieran. You know the perp?"

Kieran's eyebrows drew together with confusion as his attention shifted back to the cop. Fuck, were the guys coming out of the academy getting younger? "What the hell are you talking about, Frazier?"

"Uh, an anonymous tip came in that someone saw a male matching the perp's description argue with a woman, then slip something into her drink at Echoes. Dispatch sent me and when I got there, he was carrying her out to a truck." He shifted nervously, adding, "Along with the other man and these two women."

Kieran stared at the young cop so long that Frazier broke out in a sweat. Finally, he shook his head and said, "Christ, Frazier, don't you look at the newspaper? Your 'perp' is Dante Giancotti, and he sure as hell didn't slip my sister a date-rape drug."

The officer's mouth gaped momentarily. "Your sister?"

"Yeah." Kieran pulled Lyric into his arms and rested his chin on her head. "And this is my wife Lyric. That's my cousin Sierra, and the guy with the long hair is Dante's brother."

The cop blinked twice. "Sure, I read the papers. I just didn't make the connection when I ran the plates on the truck and it came back Giancotti Security. Damn, someone tried to set him up!"

Chapter Fourteen

Calista woke with three dachshunds snuggled against her side and Lyric propped up on an elbow and staring down at her. For a minute she stared in confusion. "Did we have a sleepover?"

Lyric grinned. "Oh yeah. And a good time was had by all—especially me, who got to referee one hell of a macho show. How do you feel?"

Calista's eyebrows drew together. Lyric wasn't making any sense. "How do I feel?"

"Still confused, I see. Go back to sleep then." Lyric rolled over and Calista heard the rustle of paper. It was enough to prompt her into sitting and taking note that Lyric was wearing jeans and a tank top while she was wearing an oversized T-shirt and panties.

"Why are you in here?"

Lyric put the newspaper down before rolling off the bed. "It was either me or World War Three was going to break out." She grinned. "I had to send the boys to their respective corners. You might have given me the heads-up about Dante and Benito. To say your brother was not thrilled to see you in their presence is a major understatement. To say he couldn't tell you'd been with both of them would be an outright lie. And to top it off, it didn't help that you were passed out and being carried into the emergency room by one of them."

Some of it started coming back to Calista, but a lot of it was missing. "I don't remember very much."

"It's probably better that you don't."

The way she said it made color rush to Calista's cheeks and her mind circle back to Lyric's earlier comment. "Did I do something…embarrassing…with Dante and Benito?" When Lyric grimaced, Calista's heart jumped. "I did, didn't I?" She frowned. "I don't remember drinking enough to get drunk."

Lyric reached over and squeezed Calista's hand. "You didn't. You were drugged. Someone slipped you some flunitrazepam. Roofies. Do you remember going to the hospital?"

"No." She tried to concentrate. "The last thing I remember was sitting at the table with you, Sierra, Dante and Benito. You took me to the hospital?"

"A little while after Dante and Benito got to Echoes."

Calista shook her head. She couldn't remember any of it. A knot tightened in her stomach. "Did I do anything embarrassing?" she asked again, unable to keep the slight quiver out of her voice.

Lyric squeezed her hand. "Not embarrassing, not really. You stood up for yourself!" She wrinkled her nose. "Well, before you got a little emotional and started crying all over the front of Benito's shirt, then got sick." Lyric gave a little laugh and leaned over to hug Calista. "Actually, I wish you could remember the part where you told Kieran that you were grown up and if you wanted to sleep with both Dante and Benito, then it was your business and he had no right to take a swing at one of your boyfriends or tell him to get the hell out of your life. That was a truly excellent moment."

Calista gave a shaky laugh and hugged Lyric back. "I said that?"

"Oh yeah."

"Did Kieran really take a swing at someone?"

"At Dante, who was definitely willing to go at it with Kieran, and probably would have if you hadn't gotten involved."

Warmth flooded through Calista, loosening the knot in her stomach. She didn't want the men in her life fighting over her, but she was honest enough to recognize that a primitive part of her was glad they were willing to do it. "Someone must have put the stuff in my drink while we were taking line-dance lessons."

"Don't go there. After Dante and Kieran finished arguing with each other, they ganged up on me. My ears are still blistered from hearing cop-delivered rants about leaving open drinks on the table unattended." She grimaced. "They've got a point. But they can't have it both ways. Either some sicko was trying to get laid, or someone was trying to set Dante up. Personally, I think it's pretty obvious this is about Dante. So it seems way more likely someone slipped the drug into your second drink before it got to our table. Until he stormed in, *I* didn't even know he was coming, so someone must have followed him and seen you. Believe me, he didn't have eyes for any other woman in the place and you might as well have had a bull's-eye on your forehead."

Calista shivered, remembering the shooting in front of Hector's Gym. "A different analogy would be a little less creepy." She smoothed a hand over each one of the dachshunds. All three of their tails wagged, though their eyes remained closed. "Guess I'd better take a shower. They're still out there?"

"Oh yeah. Tell you what. I'll talk Big Brother into driving me down to Noah's to pick up some bagels and then over to Starbucks for coffee, that'll give you some time alone with your very gorgeous men." Calista blushed and Lyric laughed. "Yep, you're definitely feeling more like yourself."

"Let me take a shower first, okay?"

"Sure."

Calista eased out of bed, feeling a little wobbly but otherwise okay. She took a minute to transfer the dogs to a round cedar dog bed next to the dresser before escaping to the bathroom and showering, brushing her teeth. Becoming human again.

She went for comfort—shorts and a loose top—but ran out of energy before she could deal with her hair. Benito took the task over as soon as she walked into the living room. "Christ, we were worried," he said, taking the brush from her hand before settling on the couch with her on his lap and Dante sitting down next to them.

Dante cupped her face, staring into it for a minute before kissing her gently. "I want you to pack up your dogs and move in with Benito until this thing with the Mitchells is over."

"I'll be okay," she said, not wanting to get into an argument with him but also knowing she wasn't going to move in with Benito. If worst came to worst, she could stay with Tyler or even one of Lyric's cousins. She liked her house and her neighborhood. She felt safe here with Tyler three doors up and Braden, Shane and Cole around the corner. And moving in with Benito, even for a few days, would just be... Her stomach flipped over. She needed to keep a little distance, a little independence until she knew where this was going.

"I don't want you here alone," Dante growled.

"We'll work it out so I won't be." She ran her finger down his nose and over his mouth. "Please, let's not fight."

Benito's arm curled around her waist, his lips brushed kisses along her neck and she relaxed against him, needing the warmth and attention. Dante groaned, moving in to cover her lips with his even as his hands burrowed under her tank top and bra to cup her breasts. "Christ, it would kill me if you got hurt because of me," he whispered before his kisses turned more aggressive, more dominant.

She whimpered underneath their onslaught and Benito's hand freed the zipper of her shorts and slipped inside, plunging into her panties and then into her slick channel. His palm rubbed against her stiff, erect clit as he stroked in and out of her, relentless in his need to pleasure her. She gave herself up to them, spasming in release as Dante captured her cry in his mouth.

He groaned then, going to his knees in front of her and pulling her shorts and panties down so he could press his face against her bare cunt, sucking and kissing, telling her with his lips and tongue how glad he was that she was okay.

She arched into him, unable to keep herself from crying out. Benito's hands moved to her breasts, the rhythm of his fondling in sync with the stab of Dante's tongue as they both drove her to orgasm again, leaving her weak and helpless against them.

With a final kiss against her pussy, Dante pulled her shorts and panties back into position before rising and leaning down so that his face was in hers. "That was to show you how happy I am you're okay. But don't think I've forgotten about your trip to San Francisco, Lista, and the punishment you've got coming."

She shivered at the promise she saw in his eyes and thought about protesting, but she knew it wouldn't do any good. And she'd just as soon not admit to visiting Morrisey, Mackall & Dekker right now.

Dante took a seat again. Benito urged her to lean forward and started brushing out her hair, gently separating the long, tangled strands, before weaving them in a French braid.

"You do that better than I do," she said, smiling as she reached back and examined his work with her fingers.

He kissed her neck, then shifted her so she was sitting sideways and he could worship her lips with his. "I love you," he whispered. "Don't scare me like that again."

Her heart felt ready to explode in her chest. She twined her arms around his neck, locking her lips to his and stroking into his mouth with her tongue.

She was only vaguely aware of a door opening, of Kieran's, "Son of a bitch!" followed by Lyric's laugh.

Reluctantly Calista pulled her mouth from Benito's, wishing she'd had time to tell him she loved him before Lyric and Kieran got back. She slid off his lap, drawn by the smell of mochas and fresh bagels.

They moved to the kitchen and Calista's thoughts went automatically to her dogs as she started to pull out plates. Lyric laughed, guessing what she was thinking. "I already fed them."

Kieran plopped down in a chair, glowering at Dante and Benito. Calista set a plate down in front of him and gave him a hug, wanting to say, *I'm an adult, deal with it*, but also wanting to avoid a confrontation. She settled for saying, "Thanks for riding to the rescue last night. I guess no one saw who actually put the drug in my drink."

Her brother's scowl moved away from the Giancottis and focused on her and Lyric. "That place is a meat market. You're not going back there again unless someone goes with you."

Calista couldn't keep a snicker from escaping when Lyric said, "By *someone*, you mean someone with a penis."

"Baby..."

Lyric rolled her eyes. "Don't start with you. I know. And don't mention Braden or Shane as possible escorts." She pulled out a bagel and tossed it to him.

Calista put plates in front of Dante and Benito, then set out some silverware before taking a seat. She had just enough time to choose a bagel and slather cream cheese on it before Kieran said, "When we're done with breakfast, I want you to pack up your dogs and some clothes and go home with Lyric. You can stay with us until this thing with Dante cools down."

Which thing? The sex? The problem with the Mitchells? Calista exchanged a smile with Lyric but unlike her sister-in-law, Calista didn't jump at the chance to get Kieran stirred up.

"Thanks, but no thanks. I'll be fine here," Calista said, giving her brother the same answer she'd given Dante, amused at how similar the two men were. This time she couldn't resist adding, "If I feel unsafe, I'll stay with Tyler."

"The hell you will," Dante growled under his breath.

They got through breakfast and Calista even managed to send the men off to their respective workplaces—but it took a promise that she and Lyric would stay together.

"Well, that was a major miracle," Lyric said, digging out a deck of cards before settling at the kitchen table and shuffling. "Up until their cars actually drove away, I didn't think they'd leave. Now we can talk about Dante and Benito. We can even play a token game of poker if you want, that'll ease your conscience since the loser has to share a sexual exploit or is forever banned from the game table."

Calista snorted. "Right. Big challenge there. I might as well spill my guts without suffering the humiliation of being whipped at poker."

"Your choice, but I'm willing to go easy on you. So is the reality as good as the fantasy?"

Calista smiled, unable to help herself. "Better." She hesitated a second, "So you've never..."

Lyric grinned. "Not from lack of fantasizing about it. I just never met the right two guys, not like you have. It takes a certain combination of personalities to pull it off. I'd say you've got that going with Dante and Benito. When we went for bagels and coffee, even Big Brother finally admitted he could see they both care about you—not that he didn't still have some choice words to say about it."

Calista grimaced. "I guess he'll share those words with me later."

Lyric's eyebrows moved up and down. "I'll do my best to take the edge off of him."

"Maybe you can tie him to the bed first and completely subdue him."

"Oh yeah, that works for me." Lyric's voice held just enough carnal knowledge to have Calista's eyes widening and her mouth forming a small "o".

"No way! Kieran? The original caveman?"

"You should try it sometime. Benito would be a perfect candidate. Practice on him, then take on Dante. There's nothing like making a tough man beg, or being on the receiving end when he gets even." Lyric grinned. "Whoever said 'paybacks are hell' must not have played the same sex games I have."

Calista nearly choked on her coffee—then spent the rest of the morning trying to squelch the erotic images that suddenly wanted to take over her thoughts.

They played poker for a while, then pulled out the case folder and went over it—not gaining any additional insight or leads.

"I guess I could always call Irene at Morrisey, Mackall & Dekker and follow up about talking to Jessica's co-workers."

Lyric settled back in her chair. "Might as well. Calling her could become your new hobby, though somehow she doesn't sound like the type you can wear down with persistence. While you're at it, why not call the fertility specialist's office? I think it's a good assumption Jessica used Dr. Lassiter. If fits with her living in a Mitchell rental apartment and working for Morrisey, Mackall & Dekker, who obviously have ties to the Mitchell family. The clinic won't give you details about Jessica, but they might give you the lawyer's name handling the adoption paperwork—it's probably someone they're connected with too. But unless the lawyer's an adoption specialist who doesn't practice any other kind of family law, it'd be hard to narrow down. It's also possible that the adopting family used their own lawyer. As far as finding Sarah Winston's grandchild, getting a lawyer name may ultimately be as far as you can take this case anyway. Then it'd be up to her whether or not she wanted to get herself a lawyer and try to open the adoption."

Calista nodded and made the calls, getting no additional information from either of them. They moved to playing Scrabble, then Yahtzee, ate lunch, and were back to poker when Calista's cell phone rang.

It was Irene Lee from Morrisey, Mackall & Dekker and she surprised Calista by saying, "I've checked around and found out the attorney's name who handled the adoption for Jessica. You should be aware, it is a closed adoption, so I can't tell you anything more than the attorney's name. I did clear it with him first. He said the adoptive parents prefer to remain anonymous, and you should inform Jessica's parents that their daughter signed away all rights to her child."

"Can you tell me whether it was a girl or a boy?"

"The attorney didn't reveal that information. Do you have a pen ready?"

Calista wrote down the attorney's name, address and phone number—not at all surprised to find him in San Francisco and in the same office building containing the offices of Morrisey, Mackall & Dekker. She followed up immediately with a call and heard the same thing from him that she'd heard from Irene. The adoption was closed, meaning even Jessica didn't know the names of the adoptive parents she had signed her child over to.

"Well, I'd say the case is closed and we should go out and celebrate," Lyric said after Calista had relayed the information, "but it doesn't feel closed, and your two macho men would probably throw a fit if we went near a bar."

Even the thought of a drink made Calista's stomach queasy. "You're right. On both counts."

Lyric dealt a couple more hands of poker, and won, before her cell phone rang. Calista only half-listened as Lyric filled Braden in on what had happened, but she perked up when Lyric said, "I think I feel an ice cream run coming on. You know the place I'm talking about... Yeah, we can take separate cars, whoever's got the tail can turn on the street right behind the shop. It's one way and there won't be much traffic on it if we head out now." Lyric flashed a grin of pure excitement at Calista. "See you in a few."

"What's going on?" Calista's stomach was jumping and twisting in reaction to the energy and anticipation sizzling around Lyric.

"Like I said, the case doesn't feel closed — despite the convenient sharing of information by Morrisey, Mackall & Dekker. Braden says he thinks someone's watching your house. He and Shane noticed two different guys in two different cars, parked at the corner today, reading. They finally had Tyler run the DMV plates. Both cars come back to Roscoe Inc. No web site. No listing in the yellow pages. The easiest way to find out if they're watching and who they're watching is to drive away and see if they follow."

"To Angel's Ice Cream Shop?"

"Yeah. I'm in the mood for chocolate. What about you?"

Calista worried her lip for a second before nodding. Lyric made being tough and fearless seem so easy, but after experiencing a drive-by shooting, then ending up in the emergency room, Calista was starting to think maybe she wasn't cut out for anything more dangerous than a kindergartener throwing a temper tantrum.

"Let me change into jeans, get my old guys inside and close the doggie door first," she said. "Then we can talk about what you guys want me to do."

* * * * *

The plan was pretty straightforward. Lyric called Braden back and got the car descriptions and license plate numbers, then gave Calista a copy of them, saying, "We leave at the same time. Braden says there's only one of them watching right now. The guy is to the left when you leave the house, in the Lexus about two blocks down. You take your Bug and go right. If he pulls out and follows you, then head for Angel's. Drive down the street behind it. Braden and Shane are on their way to get into position now. They'll trap him in there. If he doesn't follow you, stay in the general area and wait for one of us to call and tell you it's clear. You ready?"

Calista took a deep breath. "Ready."

"Try not to notice him if he gets behind you," Lyric warned before they left the house. "And don't worry. We've got you covered."

It was almost impossible for Calista not to worry—about the Lexus, which pulled out and began following her as soon as she backed out of her driveway, about Lyric. She even worried about Shane and Braden though she knew they could take care of themselves.

It also didn't help that Dante called, probably to check in on her, and she let the call go to voicemail, adding guilt on top of the worry. So that when she checked the message a moment later and heard his terse, "Baby, you and Lyric had better not be doing anything risky," her nerves tightened to the point of snapping.

But she didn't falter. They were taking chances for her, counting on her to follow through too, and for a minute she thought her emotions might spiral out of control.

Yes, she was a little afraid someone would get hurt. But it wasn't fear that had the tears threatening, it was love and gratitude. The Burkes were a fiercely loyal family. So were the Montgomerys and the Maguires. It was almost overwhelming to know she had so many people in her life who cared and would stand up for her.

The Lexus followed, usually staying four or five cars back. She tried not to look, not to do anything to tip the driver off, even though she was shaking slightly by the time she turned onto the one-way street behind Angel's.

Alley was a better description. And as soon as the Lexus made the turn after her, she saw Shane's monster truck pull in behind. Braden was waiting on the other end, and he pulled out and came to a stop, blocking the road completely.

The Lexus screeched to a halt with Shane's big-wheeled, jacked-up truck almost kissing the bumper, its height giving the impression it might climb over the car's back like a participant in a four-wheeling-bang-'em-up-derby.

Calista stopped and forced herself to get out of the Bug, though there was no way she could make herself race over to where Braden and Shane were hauling the driver out of the Lexis and spreading him against the front of his car.

Lyric squealed her Jeep to a stop next to Calista's Beetle and jumped out of the car. "Damn. They're fast!" she said before striding over to join her cousins.

Calista followed, heart racing and adrenaline surging. She'd grown up with stories of exciting "take downs", been the "criminal under arrest" from time to time in childhood play, watched more cop shows than she'd ever wanted to, but she'd never actually been involved in a real, honest-to-god action like this one.

And she wasn't sure she ever wanted to be again. But that didn't keep her from admiring Braden and Shane in motion.

They were incredible. Totally cool. Amazing.

Like Lyric's sister Erin, Braden and Shane had both ended up with the sun-kissed, California surfer, blond look. But unlike Erin, both Braden and Shane had blended the beach look with the biker look, sporting tattoos and, at least in Shane's case, a nipple ring. They were wild testosterone crossed with raw sensuality and Calista was very glad she'd never spent enough time with them to fall under their spell.

In a matter of seconds, they had the contents of the driver's wallet and glove compartment spread across the hood of the Lexus—along with a gun. "Shit," Braden said. "He's a PI!"

"Want to tell us who you're working for?" Shane asked.

"Fuck off, asshole."

Lyric snagged the driver's license. "Not very friendly, are you, Walter?" There was a definite bite to her smile. "Anyone see a permit to carry concealed?"

"Nope," Braden said. "Maybe we ought to call this in. I don't think the cops would like the look of this, a guy following a woman around with a gun."

Shane reached over, picking up the card identifying the man as a PI, and shoved it into his own back pocket. "Hell, could be a rapist for all we know. I say let him cool off at the police station, maybe see who bails him out."

Lyric nodded. "Sounds good to me. In a few minutes the men in blue will probably show up anyway. Maybe Walter here will even lose his license for carrying concealed and stalking a woman who just happens to be related to a shitload of cops. What do you think, Walter? They going to find a permit to carry concealed when they run you?"

Calista licked her lips nervously. If ever there was a time to join in, this was it. "Um, guys, really, I didn't feel threatened by him or anything. He's probably just doing his job, trying to earn a living. It's not like he's a gangster or a hit man. I'd hate to see him get in trouble...but now that I think about it, there's been another man hanging around too. I'd at least like to know who's having me watched. I'd be okay with letting him go as long as I knew that."

"Fuck!" The man struggled against the grip Braden and Shane had on him.

Lyric shrugged. "Guess that's a no." She pulled out her cell phone and opened it.

"James Morrisey," the man growled.

"And he wants you to watch Calista because...?" Lyric asked.

"How the fuck do I know? He's a fucking lawyer. Lawyers don't tell you more than they think you fucking need to know. And if you think I'll admit to telling you he's the one who hired me, you can fucking screw yourself."

Braden, Shane and Lyric exchanged glances, silently coming to an agreement. Braden said, "Since you've been so cooperative...Walter...we're going to let you go without taking the time to delay you with a flat tire. But it would be in your best interests if we don't see you again."

Lyric reached over, picked the gun up and removed the bullets, pocketing them before wiping the gun clean of prints and dropping it back on the hood of the car. Shane said, "You and Calista leave first, we'll be right behind you."

Chapter Fifteen

They joined up at another ice cream place and secured an outside table. Usually Calista would have settled for a single scoop, but after all the excitement, she went for broke — two scoops of chocolate in a waffle cone — figuring she deserved it and her nerves needed it.

"So what's the deal?" Braden said, leaning back and taking a sip of his shake. "What does James Morrisey have to gain by following Calista? So what if she's with Dante Giancotti? She could be with him and ten other guys, it's not a crime. I don't see how it plays into the Mitchell case."

Calista exchanged a look with Lyric and blushed, grateful Lyric had glossed over the more personal elements when she was bringing her cousins up to date.

Shane swirled his tongue around the top of his ice cream, flicking the tip before finally biting it. Calista's blush deepened just a little bit at the sight. Did Lyric's cousins have any idea how sinfully erotic they were? Shane's eyes met hers and she knew he noticed the blush. He grinned. "Sorry."

Calista ducked her head and concentrated on her own ice cream cone. God! No wonder Kieran went ballistic at the thought of Lyric hanging out with these two guys. They both had a wildness to them that attracted trouble, and the three of them together… They all oozed sexuality.

Not that she wasn't used to being around major doses of pheromones. Her brothers and cousins all had it, in a he-man, macho, "I've got a huge dick" kind of way. But with Braden and Shane the sensory message was more like, "ride at your own risk and be prepared to test the limits".

Her phone rang, jarring her out of her thoughts. Benito. And suddenly Calista needed to hear his voice.

"Where are you?" he asked, sounding tense.

"Eating ice cream with Lyric and her cousins."

"Which cousins?"

"Shane and Braden. They work for Crime Tells."

"Everything okay?"

"Yes." She wanted to pat herself on the back for answering so quickly and sounding so convincing. "You're still on the job?"

There was a heartfelt sigh. "Yeah, this installation is giving me some trouble. The client's paying top dollar, but he's paranoid as hell. Doesn't want anyone but me to deal with the programming, and now he wants to talk about backup systems and safe rooms. It's going to take longer than I thought it would. I just wanted to make sure you were okay."

Warmth flooded through Calista. She glanced up, wanting to tell him she loved him, but not wanting an audience the first time she said it. She had to settle for, "I'm okay."

"I better get back to work then. I love you, Lista. Stay safe."

"I could tell you the same thing."

There was a hesitation, then he laughed, a husky sound that slipped between her legs and stroked her emotion-flushed labia. "They're listening?"

"Yes."

Another husky laugh. "Are you blushing?"

"What do you think?"

"That it's one of the things I love so much about you. You're soft and real, and don't have a clue about how to hide your feelings. I'll see you later, all of you, sweetheart, without anyone else around but Dante. I need to be inside you."

"I need that too."

She closed the phone and looked up to find one knowing expression and two seriously amused expressions directed her way. Shane was the first to speak. "I notice you didn't tell Lover-boy about our little adventure."

"That's on a need-to-know basis, Shane," Braden said, "and lover-boy doesn't need to know, especially if he's like Kieran. He'd just ruin the fun." Braden took a sip of his milkshake before adding, "And I have a feeling the fun has only begun."

Lyric rolled her eyes and laughed. "And you think that because…"

"Because while everyone else has been running around like a dog chasing its tail, thinking this is all about Dante Giancotti, I have been blessed with the Maguire third eye." He sent Lyric a smirk. "Same as you have. But you're too close to this one to use it."

Lyric's eyes widened slightly, as though she was suddenly seeing some of what Braden saw. "And your gut is telling you Giancotti being involved is just a perk? That the real target here is Calista—or more accurately, what she might find out about Jessica Winston?"

Braden grinned. "You're no fun to play with, Lyric."

Shane latched on to Calista's confused expression and smiled at her before shaking his head and saying, "So for the rest of us, the poor clueless idiots who aren't blessed with the *legendary* Maguire third eye, what the hell are you two talking about?"

Braden leaned forward. "Think about it. Jessica had the baby months ago, but she was getting ready to run *now*. Where did Jessica work? Who has so conveniently provided Calista with the very information to close her case? And who set the tail on Calista?"

"Morrisey, Mackall & Dekker," Calista whispered. "I was there before going to Hector's Gym."

Lyric stabbed her spoon into what was left of her banana split. "A couple of phone calls is all it would take to find out this is Calista's first case and up until a couple of weeks ago, when school let out for the summer, she was a kindergarten teacher. The drive-by shooting followed by what happened at Echoes could have been an attempt to scare her off, or at least divert everyone's attention. The phone call giving up the information about the adoption lawyer might have closed it down as a Crime Tells' case. They were waiting to see what she'd do, whether she'd quit trying to find out more about Jessica."

"Not find out more about Jessica," Shane said. "That doesn't feel right. Think about it. Jessica's apartment was clean, right? They're defense lawyers. Big-time defense lawyers specializing in the very rich or the very famous. The only thing that makes sense is that she had something, probably something on a client, and they want it back." He frowned. "Jessica had roofies in her system when she took a header over the balcony, right?"

Calista's stomach went queasy at the mention of the drug, at how entirely helpless she'd been when it was racing through her system. Even now she could barely remember anything past Dante and Benito showing up at Echoes.

"And the police didn't recover a cell phone or keys, right?" Shane continued.

Braden tensed. "Shit. Yeah, what you're saying feels right."

Lyric nodded slightly, reaching over and squeezing Calista's hand. "From now on, you don't go anywhere alone. And we're with you on this case."

Braden tossed his empty cup, scoring a basket as it dropped into a trashcan two tables over. His grin was a sudden flash of excitement that almost made Calista want to run for cover. "Let the fun begin!"

Lyric's grin matched his and moved to include Calista. "Call Tyler, see if his PI friend in Reno confirmed Jessica was the one who rented the mailbox. And see if he can get the Nevada plate number for the Mustang. If Jessica was worried about making a quick escape, then she didn't leave her car in Reno. She left it somewhere she could get to it. Probably a covered parking garage, somewhere it wouldn't easily be seen from the street. She wouldn't count on being able to catch a flight and she wouldn't risk getting trapped at the airport."

Calista nodded slowly. It made perfect sense. It also chilled her to the core to realize that in all likelihood, Jessica Winston had been murdered. "Maybe that's why there was no key ring," she said, "or cell phone."

"Probably." Shane balled up a napkin and tossed it at the trashcan, groaning when the wind diverted it and sent it under the table. Rising from his chair to retrieve the bad throw, he said, "And that's why they've got the tail on you. They haven't found what they're looking for and they're hoping you'll lead them to it. If we had the license plate number, we could search for Jessica's car, maybe flash Jessica's picture around to some garage attendants."

Calista made the call, catching Tyler at his desk. "Will you do me a favor?" she asked.

"Anything for my favorite cook."

She smiled. His mellowness always made her feel like she really could ask him to do anything. "You're only saying that because Erin's not around."

Tyler laughed. "You're selling yourself short. Your cooking, and especially your cheesecakes, make a man never want to leave the dinner table."

"Is that a hint you expect a cheesecake later in the week?"

"I wouldn't turn one down."

"I'll make you one. Now for the favor. When you get home, would you take the boys to your house? And maybe go out with them for bathroom breaks instead of letting them use the doggie door."

"What happened?"

"Nothing. I just want to make sure they're safe."

"Where are you?"

"With Lyric, Braden and Shane."

"Let me talk to Braden."

Calista was torn between amusement and outrage. In the blink of an eye he'd gone from mellow to sounding like one of her brothers! She straightened her spine. "In a minute. First I want to know that you'll gather up my little guys and take them to your house, so I won't have to worry about them. Then I want to know if you heard back from your PI friend in Reno, and whether or not he can get the Nevada plate number for Jessica's Mustang."

There was a moment of quiet, then a laugh. "You're hanging around Lyric too much, doll. Yes, I'll haul your old men down to my place. And yes, I've heard from Jerick. He hasn't got a positive hit on the photo yet, but he already got a jump on the license plate number, figuring it'd come up sooner or later. Got something to write with?"

Calista took down the number before handing the phone off to Braden. On Braden's end there were a couple of one-word answers followed by, "Yeah, I know. It still blows my mind she married a cop. Hopefully we'll be done before he starts looking for the little wife and his baby sister."

Lyric snorted and held out her hand for the phone. Braden grinned and passed it to her. "Repeat after me, Tyler," she said. "I don't have any idea what they're up to."

Calista couldn't keep from laughing. *Oh yeah, that would go over well with Kieran.* And then she shivered, thinking about just how well it would go over with Dante and Benito.

Chapter Sixteen

It was after midnight when Calista pulled into Benito's driveway—tired and more than a little bit discouraged. She'd been so sure they were going to find Jessica's Mustang along with some answers. But they hadn't, and now she had to face Benito and Dante, knowing that neither one of them was happy about her being in San Francisco—even with Lyric, Shane and Braden.

They'd both made that clear when they called her on the cell. And they'd both guessed she was worried about something when she told them that her dogs were at Tyler's place. Calista chewed on her bottom lip, wondering how much Tyler had guessed after running the plates for Braden, and how much he'd told Dante and Benito when they went to retrieve her old guys. Her heart jumped in her chest as the front door swung open and Dante came out, waving to Braden, who'd followed her while Shane made sure Lyric got home safely.

Dante moved to the car, standing so close that when she got out, his body heat roared across her senses, sending a wave of need and a jolt of erotic fear through her. "You've got some explaining to do, then you're going to feel my hand across your ass."

She didn't protest when he made sure her car was locked before ushering her into the house. Her heart swelled in her chest when they got to the living room and she saw the dogs curled up together next to the TV, fast asleep on one of their round beds. It touched her to know Dante and Benito had made the extra effort so her old guys would be comfortable and have something familiar with them in a strange environment.

Benito rose from the couch and Calista instinctively headed for him, slipping into his arms even as his gaze met Dante's in a silent exchange over her head before Benito lowered his mouth to hers.

Calista melted into the kiss, into the security he represented. He stroked her spine, her back, pressing her tightly against his body. Telling her without words what he felt about her. But when he lifted his mouth from hers, he said, "I'm not going to stop Dante from punishing you this time, Lista. But before that happens, we're going to talk."

Nervousness settled in her stomach as Benito eased her away from his body and led her into the bedroom. Dante followed, his hand circling her arm and guiding her to the side of the bed, sitting her on the edge as they took seats on either side of her, crowding into her space but not forcing her to look at either one of them. "Let's start with something simple," Dante growled. "You went to San Francisco today because...?"

"We were looking for Jessica's car."

Benito leaned in then, rewarding her with the brush of his lips along her neck. She whimpered in response, her nipples going tight as she turned her face, wanting to feel his mouth on hers. His kiss was butterfly-soft, fleeting, and then he pulled back.

Dante's hand circled her wrist, drawing her attention to him. "And you were afraid to leave your dogs at home because...?"

She knew Dante could feel the way her pulse skyrocketed against his palm, but she tried bluffing her way past the question. "Tyler looks after them for me whenever I'm going to be really late."

Dante's expression tightened. "That little evasion is going to cost you your shirt, Lista."

Benito's hands moved to her body again, but rather than pet and stroke her, they made fast work of stripping her top off of her and leaving her chest exposed except for the delicate pink bra. She shivered, reacting to their perusal, to the way they were taking control of her.

Dante brushed his knuckles against the front clasp of the bra. "Are you going to answer the question now, or do you want to lose this too?"

She shivered again, knowing where this was leading. Unable to stop herself from wanting it. From needing them to take charge so she'd feel safe, protected, free of secrets and worry.

"Braden and Shane thought someone was watching the house. I was afraid the dogs might get hurt," she whispered, her entire body reacting to the fiercely protective look that appeared on Dante's face.

Benito's hand stroked the base of her spine, holding her in place as he rewarded her with kisses along the top of her bra, then nuzzled her nipple through the delicate fabric before pulling away from her.

"And was someone watching the house?" Dante growled.

"Yes," she whispered.

This time Benito cupped her breast and the rigid nipple stabbed desperately into his palm, making her cry out with the need to have the areola fondled and tweaked, rolled and pulled and pinched. He stroked back and forth across it once with his thumb and she arched in reaction, silently pleading for more of his praise. Benito whispered a kiss across her mouth then leaned down and did the same to her captured breast before releasing her.

"How do you know someone was watching the house?" Dante asked.

Calista licked her lips, anticipating his reaction, and decided to gloss over as much of the "take down" detail as possible. "Braden and Shane trapped him in an alley and he admitted he'd been hired to follow me."

The muscle jumped in Dante's cheek. "You were the bait?"

"Yes."

Dante leaned in and took her chin in his hand. "Baby, you know better than to try and hold out on us. You've been warned more than once. Now stand up, that's going to cost you the pants."

She obeyed, her body shaking slightly as Benito stripped off her shoes and jeans, leaving her standing in the matching bra and panties. Dante opened his mouth and she couldn't stop herself from pressing her fingers to his lips. "Please don't ask me who hired him. He'll just deny telling us, and knowing might make things more difficult for you."

For a long moment Dante sat there, letting her press her fingers to his lips. Christ, she undid him. He could read her face, see the struggle taking place there—the desire to surrender everything to them, including her worries, pitted against heart-stopping love and the belief that keeping something from him would be best.

He was completely defenseless against her. Her love burned through all his barriers, bathing him in a fire that touched every part of him, not just his cock. She tore him apart and rebuilt him into a different man—Dante smiled against her fingers—at least where she was concerned. No other woman would ever interest him again. No other woman could even hope to satisfy him. She was his. Theirs.

He wrapped his fingers around her wrist and pressed a brief kiss into her palm before pulling her hand from his mouth. "Baby, what were the ground rules we agreed on?"

Calista clamped her legs together. Her vulva was so swollen that it felt like she had a second heartbeat pulsing in her cunt and sending stabbing heat through her erect clit. She shivered, knowing they could see how stiff and hard the small organ was, how wet her panties were, how much she liked the way they punished and rewarded her, dominated her.

"What were the ground rules we agreed on, Lista?" Dante repeated, his voice like erotic sandpaper brushing over her skin.

She licked her lips. "To keep you current on where my case is heading and what I'm doing and not to go near anyone connected to the Mitchell family without one of you going with me."

Dante's hand smoothed over one hip before he hooked his thumb in her panties while Benito did the same thing on the opposite side. "You've broken both of those rules, haven't you, baby?"

"Yes." Her answer was just barely a puff of air.

They pulled the panties down and let them drop to the floor.

Benito leaned forward, teasing her clit with his tongue before tracing her slit with it, then sucking on the swollen folds of her labia. She cried out and Dante said, "That's for telling truth. Now tell us the rest of it, Lista. Who had you followed and why?"

She told them what they wanted to know, and when she was done, Benito pressed a soft kiss to her pussy in reward then stood and moved around behind her, freeing her breasts and dropping the bra on the floor as he nibbled along her neck. "Now lay across Dante's lap and take your punishment like a good girl, then we can put this behind us."

He let her go and she did what he said, positioning herself across the harsh fabric of Dante's jeans, feeling the huge bulge of his erection against her abdomen, shivering as she heard Benito's clothes hitting the floor and imagined him standing there watching, his fingers circling his cock, aroused by the sight in front of him. She whimpered and Dante's hand came down in a sharp crack across one ass cheek. "Who do you belong to?" he growled.

"To you. To both you and Benito."

His hand smoothed over the buttock before striking the other cheek. "And why do we have rules for you?"

She didn't answer quickly enough and he brought his hand down in a series of stinging spanks that had her cunt gushing and her ass lifting for more.

His hand settled, resting on her smooth buttock, intensifying the heat. "Why do we have rules for you?" he repeated before sliding his fingers between her legs, stroking her, gathering her juices then spreading her cheeks and coating her back entrance with glistening arousal, with the promise of what was going to happen next.

"So I'll be safe," she whispered.

He leaned over then and brushed kisses along her buttocks. "That's right, Lista. We care about you too much to lose you or let you get hurt." He straightened and gave her one more spank. "Now get on the bed. Lie on your back and spread your legs."

She obeyed, so aroused that it was all she could do to keep from pleasuring herself as Dante got undressed and Benito stood, waiting, face tight with arousal, his hand circling his already wet cock. She needed to be touched, but she didn't want to do anything that might lead to more punishment, not now, not when she was so close to feeling them both inside her, from being surrounded by them, comforted and protected.

She expected Benito to get on top of her, but instead it was Dante who covered her body with his, who thrust into her, making her cry out as his thick penis seated itself fully in her small channel, stretching her, touching her all the way to her soul. He groaned, thrusting once, twice, panting as though he was fighting some internal battle. And then he rolled to his back, taking her with him, his hands going to her buttocks, spreading them for his brother.

Calista's heart jumped and raced, knowing something had changed in Dante. Before now, whenever they'd taken her together, it had been Benito whose cock lodged in her sheath, Benito who kissed and soothed her, who murmured praise, who swallowed her cries of pain and pleasure as Dante took her ass, dominating her, driving all three of them to orgasm.

But this time it was Dante who murmured how much he cared. How scared he'd been when he carried her out of the bar. How he needed her to be safe because he couldn't stand the thought of not having her in his life. And finally, as their strokes became more forceful, more urgent, as the pain and pleasure blended so thoroughly that she lost herself in what the three of them had together, it was Dante who whispered he loved her.

Chapter Seventeen

She slept in until noon. And even after she woke up, she snuggled under the covers a few minutes longer, reliving what had happened, almost not daring to believe both Dante and Benito had told her they loved her.

When she finally rolled out of bed, she couldn't help but smile at the panties and bras piled on the dresser while a choice of dresses hung from the wall sconces on either side of it. She laughed. Dante and Benito were so like the men in her family.

She showered before selecting a green sundress and going in search of both her old men and her young men. She found the dogs and Benito in the kitchen.

"These guys are amazing," Benito said, looking up from where he was slicing hotdogs. "They can go from a dead sleep to begging in no time flat." He set the knife down, pulling her into his arms and giving her a lingering kiss. "I didn't know they had it in them. They've been asleep just about every time I've seen them."

"That's because I'm not big on giving them snacks between meals. I don't want them to turn into fat little walking cigars."

"You're tough." He grinned and kissed her again. "But I think the way I dispense the treats will make us all happy."

Benito scooped the sliced hotdog pieces into a bowl, then proceeded to put them around the kitchen, forcing her old men to sniff them out and get some exercise in the process.

Calista laughed. God. How could she not be madly in love with him?

When he returned to her side and set the bowl on the counter, she wrapped her arms around his waist and pulled him to her. "I love you."

He smiled, and in between kisses said, "I know. But I like hearing it all the same."

"Where's Dante?"

"In the city."

"I thought he was on administrative leave."

"He has been. But with things heating up, it looks like the department has decided it's better for all of them if he's somewhere with plenty of people to alibi him."

"Are you home for the day?"

"I'm wherever you are."

"You make it sound like I need a bodyguard."

"You're too precious to take a chance with, Lista."

She looked up at him from underneath her lashes. "You and Dante could have your choice of a thousand other women."

Benito smiled, his face so soft and open that her heart expanded to the point it almost couldn't be contained in her chest. He brushed his thumb across her bottom lip. "We could have a couple thousand other women and never care about any of them. You're perfect for us—you make us…whole…complete—fill a place that's been empty our entire lives. Loving you and being loved by you is…" he sighed and kissed her. "I can't explain it, Lista, other than to tell you no other woman has even gotten close to being important to us. Hell, our own mother never bothered to know us well enough to tell us apart. She didn't even use our names most of the time."

Calista frowned, hurting for them as though the pain was her own, and Benito laughed softly. "Don't go there. It's done. It's the past and Dante and I don't visit it. Don't hurt for us. It doesn't matter anymore. I only told you because I thought it might help you understand just how different you are for us. How intense this is." He laughed again. "How wonderful and scary it is to have someone who means so much."

They made love in the kitchen, in the bedroom, on the couch in the living room after they'd gone over the case files Dante had retrieved from her house along with her clothing.

"I can't get enough of you," Benito told her, stroking her back as she stretched out on top of him.

Calista smiled against his chest. "The feeling is mutual. But if we don't stop, I'm going to get sore again and then Dante will have to settle for blowjobs." Her face warmed against his skin just saying the word.

"Yeah, a date with your mouth will kill him. He'll hate it. Probably complain for days about being sucked off."

She snickered, pressing a kiss to Benito's chest and sitting up. "I should go back to San Francisco and keep looking for the Mustang."

Benito traced the bones along her spine. "You don't know for sure it's even in the city. It could be anywhere as long as it's close enough to public transport to get there quickly and easily. And you still don't know for sure

Jessica Winston and Lindsey Smyth are the same person—though I think you're on the right track there."

Calista sighed. "That's the trouble with this entire case. I still don't know much about Jessica."

"Talk to her mother again. Maybe Jessica had hobbies as a kid. Something that might lead you to people who knew her since the work and neighbor angles look like dead ends."

Calista nibbled on her bottom lip for a long moment. She wasn't ready to share what she'd learned with Sarah—in fact, if the truth were known, she'd just as soon leave it to Bulldog, since he had a connection with the family.

At least when she had to give parents bad news about their children's behavior or progress, there was usually plenty of warning beforehand—little notes home, phone calls, parent-teacher conferences. And even though she hated having to share bad news, it still made her feel like what she was doing was worthwhile, an investment in a child's future.

Calista sighed. She doubted anyone would ever be able to prove Jessica was murdered, though her gut told her Jessica had been. And she still hadn't resolved her own feelings about Jessica carrying a baby to term for monetary gain—because Calista was equally sure Jessica hadn't done it out of compassion for an infertile couple's plight.

"I don't think I'm cut out to be a PI," she whispered, sharing the fear she'd been harboring with Benito.

He sat up and pulled her back to his chest, hugging her to him. "Is that so terrible?"

"I don't want to let Lyric and her sisters and Tyler down. They've spent so much time getting me ready to work for Crime Tells."

He rubbed his lips along her shoulder. "Don't be silly, sweetheart. You're not going to let them down. I bet if you asked them, they'd tell you that your friendship and spending time with you is more important than whether or not you work for Bulldog. Besides, you've made a lot of progress on this case—hell, more than anyone could have expected, given the twist it's taking. See it through to the end, then decide whether you want to take on another case or go back to the classroom."

"You and Dante would rather I quit and go back to teaching."

She felt his smile against her skin. "We want you to be happy and we'll support whatever you do."

"You sound like you've been watching Dr. Phil."

He bit her shoulder gently. "Okay, the truth. Yeah, I'd rather know the scariest thing you have to face during the day is a screaming kindergartener. But that doesn't make what I said before a lie. If you want to keep working for Bulldog, then you should do it. If you want to try working in the security field, you can work at Giancotti Security and I'll train you myself—personally and very thoroughly." He kissed the spot where he'd bitten her. "If you want to teach, teach. And if, down the road, you want to stay home and take care of kids, that'd be fine too—though I wouldn't mention the baby word to Dante right now. He's already a little overwhelmed by what we've got with you."

Shock at hearing him talk about a future that included having children made Calista tense in his arms, but he took it in stride, gently chiding, "You don't think we're going to let you get away now that we've found you." He nibbled on her earlobe. "I love you. Now get dressed before I fuck you again. Make your phone call and see if you can learn more about Jessica."

She got dressed and made the phone call, but was left with only a depressing snapshot of Jessica's childhood.

"Didn't sound like it went anywhere," Benito said when she hung up.

Quite frankly, Calista, my daughter was a secretive, slothful child. Unlike her sister and brother, nothing seemed to interest Jessica beyond clothing and being associated with the right crowd. Those things are important, of course, but there was nothing beyond that. No ambition to excel or succeed or accomplish something noteworthy. Her brother was an outstanding baseball player growing up and is now an advertising executive on the fast track. Her sister is finishing up her last year of med school at Harvard.

"No, it didn't." She dialed Tyler. "Anything on the mailbox in Reno?" she asked when he answered.

"You're the second person today to ask me that question. But at least with you, I don't have to worry you're going to try and break into it."

"Lyric called?"

"Yeah, in the company of Braden and Shane—which is like leaving matches stored with the dynamite."

Calista laughed. "And what did you tell her?"

"The truth at the time, which was no. But I just got back to my little cubicle here among the men and women in blue and found a voicemail from Jerick. He got a positive ID from the guy who actually rented the box to Jessica a.k.a. Lindsey Smyth."

"What would it take to get into it?"

"The easiest way is a key. The place is self-serve. Jerick said you should be looking for a key that's very similar to a post office box key. The engraving on it will start with the letters MBAU23 followed by a dash and a bunch of numbers."

"So it all comes back to the car. If Jessica was really heading to Hawaii, she wouldn't have rented another apartment somewhere. She would have stayed in hotels if she couldn't go back to her place."

"Probably."

"Thanks, Tyler."

She started to call Lyric, but before she could, Laura, James Morrisey's personal secretary at Morrisey, Mackall & Dekker, called. "Are you available to meet with Mr. Morrisey this afternoon with respect to Jessica Winston?" she asked.

Nerves rippled through Calista's stomach at the prospect of meeting with the lawyer who'd hired someone to follow her. "Of course. I can be there in an hour and a half."

"I'll tell him. There's parking for our clients in the garage under the building."

Calista hung up. "I need to go to the city."

"Who was that?"

She told Benito and watched his face grow every bit as hard as Dante's. "I'm going with you." There wasn't room for any negotiation in his voice.

"Just as far as the parking garage." His face tightened. She put her hand on his chest. "You can walk me to the elevator and I'll go straight up and come straight back down after the meeting. Nothing's going to happen to me, but I need to do this by myself, and it would probably be better for Dante if you weren't seen in Morrisey, Mackall & Dekker's office." A muscle twitched in Benito's cheek, the first time she'd seen it in him, though she'd seen it plenty of times in Dante. She almost smiled. Instead she leaned forward and kissed him. "Please, let me do this."

He rubbed his mouth against hers. "Dante'll probably kill me."

Chapter Eighteen

She knew what James Morrisey looked like from seeing clips of him on TV and in the newspapers. Confident, handsome, photogenic — a charismatic man who'd come from an old, wealthy San Francisco family himself. But the pictures hadn't captured the underlying ruthlessness of the man — the commitment to do what needed to be done on behalf of his clients. He was a shark who would scent the smallest drop of blood and attack.

"Please have a seat," he said, not bothering to rise from his own chair behind the desk, not bothering to offer a handshake or anything to drink.

She settled in a chair, aware of the psychological game he was playing and trying not to react to it — praying that some of the hours and hours of poker would pay off and she'd be able to bluff her way through this meeting or at least keep from giving anything away.

Morrisey steepled his hands together and rested his chin on his fingertips, lancing her with cold blue eyes and a condescending smile. "I'm sure we'd both agree, Calista," he said, using her name in a way that made her think of a small child sent to the principal's office, "that Jessica Winston's parents are better off not knowing the true details of their daughter's life. I'm certainly willing to grant you access to some of her co-workers, but they'll tell you the same thing I will. Jessica wanted wealth and the finer things it brings, but she didn't want to work for it, and her secretive, greedy nature made her an unattractive candidate for marrying into it. As you've already surmised, she found a unique way to use her body to provide her with an income. That being said, we've done what we can to provide you with the information you need in order to give her family closure, and yet you're continuing to pursue the matter."

Calista stiffened slightly as he opened a desk drawer, some sixth sense filling her with dread when he pulled out a manila envelope and placed it on the desk in front of him.

"There are confidentiality laws in place to guard conversations between lawyers and their clients. Even the great unwashed masses in our society seem to have grasped that fact." He smiled, a flash of strong white teeth that threatened rather than reassured. "And you certainly don't fall in those ranks. I understand you're an educator, a woman entrusted with our youngest school children. Kindergarteners, I believe. An interesting mix, being a teacher and also a private investigator, though I imagine working for and with your in-laws provides a certain amount of entertainment while you're out on summer break." His eyebrows rose and his fingers lightly tapped the manila envelope. "Since you haven't yet turned in your resignation, I assume you're planning to return to the classroom in the fall."

"I haven't made up my mind yet," Calista said, trying to sound casual but knowing she hadn't pulled it off nearly as well as Lyric would have.

"Ah, I see. I imagine there are still moral clauses in teacher's contracts, but that's not my area of the law. Well, I'm sure you'll do what's best for everyone involved." He opened the folder then and extracted the contents, spreading the three eight-by-eleven photos on the desk so Calista could see them.

Her eyes went instantly to the first one, a shot capturing the front of her house, identifying it by the house number, though she didn't need the address to recognize her home — nor did she need the time and date stamp in the bottom right corner to recognize when the photograph had been taken.

The gauzy curtains made it impossible to positively identify the three people in the photograph, but there was no question as to what they were doing. She couldn't keep the heat from rising to her face as she remembered what had transpired while Kieran and Lyric were out getting bagels and coffee.

Two men and a woman. Dante's back was to the window as he knelt in front of her, his face buried in her cunt while Benito pressed kisses along her neck and cupped her breasts.

Though it wasn't conclusive evidence, it was damning. The second photograph panned the front of the house, capturing her car and both of theirs, while leaving the figures in the living room only shadows behind the curtain. The third photograph, taken during the previous night, showed all three cars parked at Benito's house.

Without a word, Morrisey collected the pictures and returned them to the envelope, leaving it in front of Calista. "They're yours if you wish to take them." A quick check of his watch. "I need to leave for court. As I said earlier, Jessica Winston's parents are better off not knowing the true details of their daughter's life, but I'm certainly willing to grant you access to some of her co-workers if you still feel the need to talk to them. And should you stumble across anything belonging to

Morrisey, Mackall & Dekker, I certainly hope you'll return it to us. The law is quite clear on lawyer-client privilege. Goodbye, Calista, I hope the next time we meet it'll be under more pleasant circumstances." His smile didn't even make an attempt to reach his eyes.

She picked up the envelope and left without saying anything, wishing she was more like Lyric, Braden or Shane, wishing she could have said something, done something, instead of sitting quietly and letting him deliver his blows. But even in the safety of the elevator, she couldn't come up with any other scenario than the one that had taken place. She wasn't like Lyric. Never would be. But that didn't mean she wasn't a fighter in her own right.

Calista stiffened her back and tried to school her features so Benito wouldn't know something was wrong. She'd tell him and Dante about the photographs and the implied threat, but not now. Not until she'd had a chance to talk to Lyric about it.

Benito was out of the VW and striding toward her as soon as she got close to the car. "What happened?" he asked, his voice a rough, protective growl as he pulled her into his arms and trapped the folder between them.

"Nothing terrible." *Not yet.* "He pretty much confirmed indirectly that Jessica had taken something from a client's file and that she was the type of woman who liked money but didn't want to work for it. He was careful though, not saying anything up front, not mentioning blackmail, but implying a lot."

Benito eased back and looked into her face. "He upset you."

She closed her eyes, fighting the mix of emotion trying to overwhelm her. She was trying not to be afraid of the future, trying to come to grips with having her privacy violated, with being threatened with the loss of her teaching job. "I'm okay," she whispered, leaning in and resting her forehead on his chest. "I'm just not cut out for this kind of work." She rubbed against his shirt. "I need to find Lyric and talk to her. Okay?"

"Anything, sweetheart. You know I'd do anything for you, don't you?"

She lifted her head and opened her eyes, letting the love she saw in his fill her with confidence, with security, with resolve to see this through to the end and to keep Dante and Benito from knowing about the blackmail attempt, at least until she was sure they wouldn't do anything hasty—a small smile played across her lips—like beat the crap out of James Morrisey.

Benito kissed her, his lips quirking up slightly, some of the worry gone from his eyes. "Better now?"

Calista laughed. "Amazing what one of your hugs and kisses will do, huh? Maybe *you* should be a kindergarten teacher kissing away owies."

"No thanks. The only owies I want to kiss are yours. Still need to talk to Lyric?"

"Yes."

"Okay, let's find her then."

* * * * *

Lyric was a lot closer than they expected. She was across the bay, in Oakland. "You got the PI sixth sense going," she said as soon as she answered her phone. "The boys and I have been checking out parking garages near

BART stations all morning. We just found the Mustang. You with Benito, or Dante?"

"Benito."

"Good, this is no time to have a cop around."

Calista grimaced. God, Kieran would kill her if he knew she hadn't tried to stop Lyric from breaking into Jessica's car. "Lyric…"

Her sister-in-law laughed. "I've got Shane and Braden with me. It's almost too easy. We'll meet you on the street in front of the parking garage and you can give us a lift back to the BART station. We left our cars there and hoofed it, same as Jessica would have been doing. You get a whole different perspective when you're on foot."

Calista nibbled her bottom lip, feeling guilty about leaving the risky part to Lyric and her cousins — even though she knew they *loved* taking those kinds of chances. "I should…"

"Too late. Shane just popped the trunk. Gotta go or they won't leave any fun for me." She gave Calista directions and hung up.

"She found the car?" Benito asked.

"They did. She's with Shane and Braden." Calista passed on the directions.

Benito took her hand, entwining his fingers with hers. "I know you wish you were more like her, but I'm glad you're not. You're exactly right for us. Lyric'd be a hell of a lot of work." He grinned. "Though I've gotta admit, Dante and I are going to enjoy watching the show, seeing her put your brother through his paces."

Heat seared through her heart and belly at the way he so easily acknowledged a future that held all three of them. "I love you," she blurted out.

He laughed, giving her hand a light squeeze. "Damn, wish we'd brought the truck. Then we could have taken a scenic drive and found a place to pull over and try out the backseat."

* * * * *

Shane, Lyric and Braden were an amazingly tight fit in the back of the Beetle, but somehow they managed it, crowding in almost as soon as the Bug came to a stop.

"Hit it," Braden said, grinning and laughing so Calista didn't really think they were being chased by security officers or cops.

Calista turned to look at Lyric. "Find anything?"

"A key in the ashtray along with road maps for Mexico and a bunch of real estate brochures for oceanfront property there—which makes me think Jessica's call to her mother and the conversation about Hawaii were just in case something went wrong with her blackmail plan and the lawyers called in favors and sent some of their less reputable clients looking for her. There was also a folder of newspaper clippings along with a Nevada driver's license issued to Lindsey Smyth." Lyric handed the key and the file to Calista. "Take a guess which case our girl was following."

Excitement and foreboding tangled into a ball of nerves in Calista's stomach. "The Mitchell case." She saw Benito's hands tighten on the steering wheel.

"Yeah, right from the start. And behind those clippings are a bunch of them from a couple of years back. Ever hear of Sammy "The Source" Miyabe?"

Calista's eyebrows drew together in a frown. "The name sounds familiar, like someone my dad or my uncles talked about at the dinner table."

"Sounds about right. Sammy The Source got hauled in for using high school kids to traffic date rape and party drugs, including ecstasy and roofies. He turned state's evidence—in Florida and New York—then went into Witness Protection. Some of the cases are probably still working their way through the court system."

"Shit," Benito said. "The same drugs found in Jessica's system. She must have found a link between Sammy The Source and the Mitchell kids."

Lyric grinned. "Makes sense to me. Otherwise why would she have the clippings all in the same tidy little file? It also explains why she was being careful. Hard to know what kind of connections Sammy still has, and the Mitchell kid and his friend come from enough money to buy a lot of protection. Ten to one, whatever she has linking them all together is in her Reno mailbox."

Calista turned the key over in her hand and saw the engraved letters and numbers. MBAU23. "Tyler's PI friend said the mailbox key would look like this."

"We could get to Reno and back well inside of ten hours," Shane said, "even stopping for gas, food and a couple of hands of poker."

Benito pulled into the BART parking lot and Lyric directed him to where they'd left her car. "I need to talk to you," Calista said as they stopped.

The men got out and moved away, taking up positions against the Jeep while Lyric climbed into the driver's seat next to Calista. "What's up?"

Calista told her about the meeting with James Morrisey, handing Lyric the manila envelope and watching as Lyric's eyes narrowed when she studied the photographs it contained.

For a long minute Lyric said nothing, then she put the pictures in the envelope and asked, "What do you want to do about this?"

Calista took the envelope back and slipped it under her seat, grateful once again that Benito hadn't asked about it, but had silently given her the space she needed in order to sort things out for herself. "I want to see this through to the end, but I also don't want to do anything that will ruin the case against the Mitchell boy and his friend. If the case gets thrown out, then everything Dante's been through will be for nothing."

Lyric smiled, a shark's smile that could rival Morrisey's, though hers was edged with excitement and pure amusement. "I've got an idea, but because of certain...restrictions...Kieran's got on me, you'll have to be the one to see it through."

Calista was almost afraid to ask, but she did anyway. "What do you have in mind?"

"Celine VanDenbergh."

Nervousness rolled over Calista like an ice-cold wave just hearing the name. Lyric had tangled with the newspaper reporter and suspected animal rights extremist on the dachshund case.

"You think she'll dig up the connection and do a story on it?"

"Oh yeah. She'll run with it."

"I thought her passion was animal issues."

"It is. But this story has three elements she won't be able to resist. A connection to the Montgomerys. A chance to stick it to the rich and privileged. And the opportunity to score a big one against the Feds." At Calista's surprised expression, Lyric's smile widened. "Hey, just because your brother says she's off-limits doesn't mean I don't know a lot about her. Her office isn't too far away, we could swing by before heading to Reno."

"Do you think Morrisey still has people following me?"

"I doubt it. He probably thinks he's played his ace and you've folded."

"Let's do it then," Calista said, her heart jolting with nervous excitement while her stomach felt like someone had aimed a blowtorch at it.

Lyric started the car, easing off the brake and hitting the gas. "Braden's got a set of my car keys, not that he needs them to take the Jeep. Call one of them and tell them we're running an errand. Tell them to meet us at the Public Market in Emeryville. We can head for Reno from there."

Calista called Benito, wanting to blurt out where they were going but forcing herself to tell him that she'd explain later, when they were on the way to Reno. As she closed the cell phone, Lyric said, "You should go through the file and make sure you know what you're passing on to Celine."

Something in Lyric's voice tipped Calista off and she went through the file carefully, making sure to examine each article carefully. Toward the back she found it—a small, clipped birth announcement from a Carmel newspaper a couple of months earlier celebrating the addition of a baby girl to the family of Franklin and Marie Faulkner.

Without a word, Calista removed the clipping and put it in her glove compartment, knowing by Lyric's silence that the choice was hers about what to do with the information.

"Play your hand close to your chest, and don't be afraid to fold," Lyric warned a few minutes later when she pulled over to drop Calista off.

Despite the nerves racing along her spine, Calista laughed. How many times had she heard those sayings while she was learning to play poker?

Celine VanDenbergh was almost mannish—with a narrow, hawkish-face and brown-gray hair cut in a severe style. Lyric had told Calista once that the reporter reminded her of a bird of prey. It was an accurate description.

"So you're Lyric's sister-in-law," Celine said, rising from behind her desk and offering a firm, no-nonsense handshake. "Here on your own, or is she around somewhere?"

"She suggested I pass this off to you," Calista said, handing Jessica's folder to the reporter but not admitting Lyric was nearby.

Celine set the folder on her desk and opened it, quickly moving through the clippings as a small smile played at the edges of her lips. "Your boyfriend?" she asked, returning to the front of the file where there was a picture of Dante.

"A friend."

Celine tilted her head, a birdlike gesture that made Calista stiffen. "His brother owns a security company."

A shiver passed along Calista's spine and without a word she reached for the file. She didn't want Benito tangled up with the Animal Freedom Front.

Celine's hand came down on Calista's, trapping it against the folder. "You guys are all straight shooters. It's a pain in the ass, but it's also what I like about you. The story is juicy enough. There's no ante to play." She took her hand off Calista's and fished out a business card, scribbling on the back. "Send anything else you get to this e-mail address."

* * * * *

After everything else that had happened, the trip to Reno and getting into Jessica's mailbox were almost anticlimactic—not that Calista minded. She'd had enough excitement to last for a while.

She glanced at Benito, glad he was here to share this moment with her. He leaned in and gave her a kiss before they both turned their attention to the papers and photos that had probably gotten Jessica killed.

"They'll never be able to prove Jessica was murdered," Braden said, voice and manner serious for a change as they sat around the table at Starbucks, "but this is enough to make it worth someone's money to have it done."

Calista studied the photocopies Jessica had somehow managed to acquire. It gave her the creeps and made her sad at the same time to think about high school kids like the Mitchells and their friends—kids who had more opportunity than any of the kids she came in contact with — calling themselves the High Boyz Club and making a fortune selling rave drugs and date-rape drugs.

But it was all there, laid out in a conversation between Paul Mitchell and James Morrisey. They'd gotten the idea of forming the club and selling the drugs from a friend of theirs at school, a boy they knew as Peter Goss, a boy whose father was a golf buddy with their father.

If Paul knew there was a connection to Sammy The Source, he didn't admit to it, so they could only guess how Jessica had found it. But there was no doubt. She had.

Calista turned her attention to the two photographs that had also been in the mailbox. The first was a group of men around a golf cart. She recognized James Morrisey right away and shivered. Eric Mitchell was there too, along with Perry King, the father of the other boy who'd been present at the shooting. And sitting in the golf cart was Dr. Robert Lassiter.

Lyric reached over and tapped a man holding his drink up in a toast. "This looks like Sammy, plus about ten years and minus a couple thanks to plastic surgery."

"Got it in one," Braden said, leaning closer. "I don't see anything privileged about this photo. Could have found it in Jessica's apartment. We should find a place where we can scan it into a computer. I'm sure Calista can think of someone to e-mail it to, in addition to Crime Tells."

They moved to the second picture. This one was easy to identify as a high school yearbook shot with a cluster of students. The Mitchell brothers were easy to spot. Benito tapped a face. "Looks like a younger version of Sammy The Source. I bet this is Peter Goss."

"Yeah," Shane said. "Like father, like son."

Braden grinned. "No harm, no foul scanning this picture and sending it on its way, too. Let's do it."

Chapter Nineteen

Benito and Calista got in late and found Dante already there. He opened the front door and stood, framed by the light, hands on his hips, his pose casual, though Calista could see the tension and need vibrating off him. She nibbled on her bottom lip and looked around nervously, suddenly anxious about having more photos taken of the three of them together — of her with either of them.

"What's wrong?" Benito asked, picking up on her worry.

She broke down then, unable to put her fears into words, unable to shun either one of them by avoiding their touch. With shaking hands Calista retrieved the folder from underneath the seat and handed it to him. Benito opened the car door so the overhead light would go on.

His face went from worried to dangerously pissed as soon as he saw the photographs. "James Morrisey threatened you with these?"

She nodded, tears forming as the roller coaster of emotion from the last few days caught up with her. "I don't want to hurt either of you. But I don't want any more pictures."

"Don't cry, Lista, please don't start — at least until we get inside and I can hold you. Okay?

Her throat was suddenly tight and raw. "Okay."

"Let's go then. I'll stay between you and Dante until we get into the house. I don't think there's anyone doing surveillance, but we won't risk any more photographs. All right?"

"I don't want to show him the pictures. Not yet. Not until we see what Celine does with the information we gave her."

A muscle ticced in Benito's cheek. "We'll see. Now let's go or he's going to storm out here."

They made it inside, behind closed doors, but not without Dante knowing something was wrong. "What the hell is going on?" he demanded, glaring at Benito and hauling Calista up against him so that his erection pressed aggressively into her abdomen. "You guys have been all over the map today and you won't tell me a goddamn thing." There was anger in his voice, but hurt too at being left out.

The tears that had been threatening in the car chose that moment to escape. "Fuck," Dante growled, "don't start, Lista." He gave her a little shake, then hugged her tight. "Don't you dare."

His panic at having her start crying in his arms derailed the tears, making Calista choke out a mangled laugh before touching her lips to his. "I love you."

Goddamn, he couldn't take much more of this. It had made him crazy being trapped in the city and knowing they were both out there, digging around in a case that kept getting more and more dangerous. Fuck, not that he didn't trust Benito to do his best to keep her safe, he did. But what if there was another drive-by shooting and he lost both of them?

A fist tightened around Dante's heart and he took her mouth aggressively, using his tongue to duel with hers, to rub and twine and dominate until she whimpered and softened and begged with her body for him to take her.

Christ, he'd meant to get some answers, but now the only thing he wanted was to claim her in the most primitive way a man can claim his woman, by shoving his cock into her while another man watched. Fuck, he couldn't seem to stop himself from ripping her panties off, from growling out commands, ordering her to get on her hands and knees as he shot Benito a desperate look that had his brother opening the front of his own pants and moving in front of Calista so that she could take his cock into her mouth while Dante fucked her.

God. She killed him. The sight of her mouth on Benito, of her still wearing her heels, her dress shoved up and her ass in the air, legs spread, vulva rosy and swollen and wet while her thighs glistened with arousal almost made him come in his pants. Fuck, he needed her.

"God, Lista, I love you," he said, freeing his penis and ramming himself into her tight little channel. Son of a bitch, he felt like a caveman around her. All he could think about was rutting on her until neither of them could move.

His breath heaved in and out in sharp pants, his body so tense that there was no way he could take it slow and easy. He groaned again, giving up any semblance of control as he began fucking her.

Her cries, the way her body yielded underneath him to the sound of flesh slapping against flesh, to the feel of his balls striking her bare pussy, all drove him higher, sending him into a desperate race for release.

He pressed hot, sucking kisses along her neck and shoulders as his fingers took possession of her clit, claiming it just as he claimed every other part of her, using it to give her pleasure, to make her scream out and tighten on his cock as she orgasmed, milking him of his seed in the process.

Fuck, she was his own personal heaven.

* * * * *

Calista woke to the sound of male voices murmuring in the other room. Heat exploded in her heart, in her womb. If felt so right to wake up like this, with the memory of their touch and their words of love fresh in her mind. To know they were close by.

She stretched and got out of bed, smiling at how well-loved her body felt, at how even now her breasts and cunt were swelling in anticipation of greeting Dante and Benito. She delayed long enough to take a quick shower and braid her hair before pulling on a dress, unable to stop herself from laughing and silently promising to go by her house and get some shorts and jeans.

"Is there coffee?" she asked, kissing Dante first since he was closer, then moving to Benito and doing the same.

"I'll get you some," Benito said. "Go look at the paper." But he stopped her when she would have moved away, kissing her again before adding, "I brought him up to date about everything."

Calista returned to the table and settled next to Dante. He flipped the paper back to the front page, saying, "When you know where the bones are buried, it's easy to dig them up."

And it doesn't hurt to have the intel capabilities of the Animal Freedom Front behind you, Calista thought, remembering how often she'd heard Kieran say he'd rather take on organized crime than the AFF cell Lyric had tangled with.

Juicy was a good word for the story. Not only was there an identification of Sammy "The Source" Miyabe—tying him to the hottest new party drug to hit the streets and linking him to the Mitchell case—but there was a scathing exposé on how the Feds involved in keeping Sammy safe had looked the other way rather than come forward and reveal he was back in business again, this time while under government protection.

Lyric had called it right.

Celine had pulled out all the stops, sticking it to the rich and privileged and scoring a big one against the Feds.

Calista smiled. She owed Lyric a huge hug.

Benito set her coffee down in front of her and settled in the chair beside her, drawing her attention to him and to Dante. Make that at least two huge hugs and a night on the town.

From the day Lyric's life had intersected with the Burke family, none of them had been the same.

"Not bad work for your first case," Benito said.

She worried her bottom lip for a second before saying, "My first and last, I think."

"Good," Dante grunted and she laughed.

"I guess you don't watch Dr. Phil," she said, and the look on his face made her lean forward and kiss him. "Never mind, I love you just the way you are."

Benito ran his fingers down her spine, making her shiver as blood rushed to her labia. "There's a good chance James Morrisey won't bother doing anything with the photographs," he said, and the warmth she'd been feeling disappeared in a heartbeat. "He doesn't have anything to gain from it, and he'd end up pissing off a lot of people—including cops—which wouldn't be a good thing to do at a time like this, when people are going to wonder what the parents of those kids actually knew. As soon as this mess settles down, Dante's going to quit. He's always owned half of Giancotti Security. We've got work in Nevada and Southern California, but we could go anywhere." He paused and whispered kisses along her neck before adding, "Marry one of us, Lista. And if you're worried about living here, about the truth of how it is between us coming out, then pick a city and we'll buy a house there. It doesn't matter where we live as long as we've got you."

Chapter Twenty

Calista packed up her dogs and went home.

She needed time to think.

Time to come to terms with an offer as scary as it was exciting.

She needed space to sort out if she really had enough courage to openly embrace a lifestyle that included both men. Not that they would flaunt it, but there was no way to completely hide the love and affection between them, and no matter where they lived, there would eventually be rumors.

She also had to close out the case by meeting with Bulldog.

Calista agonized over what to tell him, but in the end, she went to the office without the birth announcement for Melissa Marie Faulkner.

It was her call, and she made it—not without a lot of soul searching and not without an ache in her heart and a question in her mind whether it was the right one.

But in the final analysis, she decided her duty to Sarah Winston ended with providing the name of the attorney who'd handled the adoption.

Lyric came by later, bringing Starbucks and giving Calista a hug before saying, "Bulldog told me. Don't sweat it. This was all about trying something new and meeting men who weren't divorced fathers, married fathers or lecherous fathers. Right? I'd say it was a rousing success even if once was enough." She grinned. "Damn, you blew the case out of the water and you ended up with Dante and Benito. Does it get any better than that?"

Calista worried her lip for a second before blurting out, "They want me to marry one of them but live with both of them. Dante's going to quit the force and work with Benito. They're willing to live anywhere I want to live."

Lyric's eyebrows shot up and for once Calista thought maybe she'd actually managed to shock her sister-in-law. She should have known better.

"Why only one of them? Marry them both. Have kids. If you dressed Dante and Benito the same and cut their hair alike, they're identical or close to it. It's not like any kids you have would obviously belong to one or the other."

Calista's heart raced and fantasies rushed in. She tried to squelch them by saying, "Last I heard, it's against the law to marry two men in all fifty states, and probably most of the world."

Lyric only lifted an eyebrow, as if to say, "So?"

Calista laughed. "Oh yeah, I forgot who I was talking to."

Lyric shrugged. "You ever meet my friend Magic? He's got a license to perform ceremonies. He'd do a private one marrying you to both Dante and Benito. Then you could choose between them and have a public ceremony if you wanted."

Calista's hands shook slightly as she lifted her mocha to her lips. Lyric made it sound so reasonable, so possible—but... "And what about my family?"

"I didn't say it was going to be easy," Lyric admitted. "Some of them will probably figure it out, some of them you might tell, some will happily remain in denial and some will disapprove or be disappointed in you. But there are a couple of things I've noticed about the Burkes—one, they're big on family, which means they'll still love you even if they think you've gone completely crazy—and two, the men in your family all have a major macho complex going. They're going to feel protective and they're not going to like Dante and Benito hanging around you, because they're going to think the worst—here are these two guys messing with their sister, daughter, cousin, et cetera—taking advantage of her, using her. But if you were married to Dante, for instance, then the ball would be in his court, he'd be *the man of the family*, and it'd be his problem if you were sleeping with his brother."

Calista couldn't help but laugh at Lyric's accurate representation of the Burke men. The only thing saving them from being complete cavemen was that they loved deeply and were completely loyal and honorable. True, they'd tell you what you should do with your life, whether they liked your friends or not, what to wear and anything else they got into their macho minds, but they'd catch you when you fell, commiserate with you when you got hurt, kick ass if needed—and take you out for chocolate if you'd promise not to cry anymore.

"I'll think about it," she told Lyric, forcing the words out, making them a promise so she wouldn't chicken out.

Go for the gusto. Look where it had taken her so far. Look where it might still take her.

Lyric left a little while later, and Calista called, inviting Benito and Dante over for dinner.

She'd planned on sharing Lyric's idea while they ate by candlelight. But her quick departure from their house — with her dogs — must have spooked them because neither Benito nor Dante mentioned the earlier conversation, and yet both of them were so attentive and gentle it almost made her start crying.

God, they'd probably make her crazy, but she couldn't imagine a life that didn't include both of them.

They ended up making love, an intense round of sex that made it seem like they'd been apart for days instead of just since the morning. Afterward Calista lay between them, her head on Benito's shoulder, her leg thrown over his, her cunt pressed against his hip while Dante pressed his front to her back, resting an arm on her side while his hand cupped her breast.

"Lyric came by earlier today. She's got a friend who would perform a private ceremony marrying me to both of you. I know it wouldn't be legal, but — "

Benito's smile cut her off. "Are you asking us to marry you?" She couldn't stop the blush from stealing over her face and Benito laughed. "God, Lista, there's no way you're ever getting away from us. Set a time and place and we'll be there wearing tuxes if that's the way you want it." He kissed her.

Dante adjusted their positions, maneuvering her so she was on her back with his face above hers. "I still want to make it legal," he said, giving her a kiss every bit as gentle and loving as Benito's. "We can hit the Justice of the Peace before or after, but you've got to officially marry one of us, Lista."

She started to say, *Which one of you?* but then thought about how the Montgomerys and the Maguires determined everything from who was going to be lead on a case to who was making the Starbucks run. "So we'll play poker to figure out who the lucky groom is?"

Dante laughed. "Hell no. Marry Benito. You're his personal magnet. He can't be in the same room with you without being pressed up against you or kissing you. That'd be a little tougher for people to ignore if you were legally my wife."

Calista studied Dante's face, looking for shadows that would tell her he was worried about being on the outside looking in, but all she saw was love and amusement. "You're sure?"

"Yeah, baby, I'm sure. You belong to both of us. Alone or together. A piece of paper and a ceremony don't make it any more real."

Enjoy this excerpt from
Cady's Cowboy
© Copyright Jory Strong, 2005

Kix laughed softly at the challenge she'd just issued. He couldn't wait to get her underneath him. Hell, he couldn't wait to get her on top of him. He'd give her a no-holds-barred ride that she wouldn't get anywhere else. Damn, but she was driving him crazy.

Truth be told, he hardly had to lift a finger and the women came running. Between being the sheriff and being part of the Branaman clan, he almost had to use the nightstick to beat them off.

There'd been a couple of fillies along the way who'd tried to play hard-to-get, but Cady was the real deal—a heap of honesty laced together with sensuality. She'd probably be a hellcat in bed—with the right man. And he was planning to be that man.

Kix grinned. She felt the attraction, he'd bet his favorite truck that her cunt was all slicked up and waiting for him. And her nipples—they'd been as hard as his cock from the moment Adrienne had introduced them. Now he just had to get her to stop dancing out of reach and accept what was going to happen between them.

"Not a bad lead, darlin'. The Weasel sounds like a good man to talk to," Kix said when they were on their way to the racetrack. He couldn't resist the temptation to lean closer and brush the wild curls back from her face.

For a split second she allowed the touch, then color rushed to her face and she jerked away from him. "Do you think you could stay on your side of the truck?"

"I reckon I can try if you really want me to."

Cady risked a glance in his direction and immediately wished she hadn't. He was just…too masculine…too sexy…too adorable…too everything…and definitely too much for her. "Are you sure you're really a sheriff?"

"Yeah, been one for the last five years." He grinned and she was immediately entranced by the sparkle in his eyes and the little dimple next to those kissable lips. His eyebrows moved up and down. "You want me to bring out the handcuffs, or do you want to move right to the nightstick?"

Cady forced her eyes back to the road though she had a harder time forcing erotic images of being cuffed to the bed out of her mind—not that she'd ever even come *close* to experiencing that fantasy, but with Kix—whoa, *nix* that. She was *not* going to get involved with him. He was trouble with a capital H for heartbreak.

When they got to Bay Downs, Cady pulled out her camera and made sure she had release forms along with film. Besides being a great cover for investigating, she genuinely loved photography—it was one of many things she had in common with Erin and Lyric.

Kix quirked an eyebrow. "No digital camera?"

"Not on Bulldog's cases. He wants to have negatives."

Kix picked up her camera case and studied the laminated business card glued to the front. "Cady Montgomery, Professional Pet Photography." He grinned. "This for real?"

"Yes." Cady cringed inwardly when she heard the defensiveness in her voice.

"Would have pegged you for a doer instead of a looker."

"What does that mean?"

A slow grin settled on Kix's face. Damn if she wasn't as prickly as a hedgehog. "I'm just surprised you're a picture taker. Way I've always seen it, there are two kinds of people—those that stand around watching life go by and those that take it by the horns and ride it for all it's worth."

Cady frowned at him. "A person *can* be a professional photographer and live life to the fullest, just like a person *can* be good at multiple things. Not everyone" — her eyes conveyed a silent *like you* — "is good at only one thing. I'm also a good PI and a damn fine poker player."

His laugh stroked right over her. "Well darlin', I'm good at a lot of things, too. In fact, I've been known to play a mean game of strip poker, myself. Maybe later we can see who's better — just to set the record straight."

Before she could stop herself, Cady's eyes dropped to the still very noticeable bulge in his jeans. "Pass."

Kix chuckled. "Darlin', at least hesitate for a minute before you slam my ego."

Her eyes moved back up his body until she met his gaze. God, he was hard to resist. She was a sucker for men who had a sense of humor and didn't take themselves so seriously. "I'll bet you weren't even raised on a ranch. You probably grew up in the city watching westerns."

Kix slapped his hand on his chest. "Darlin', you wound me. I was born and raised on the Kicking A Ranch — home of fine horses, fine cattle and mighty fine men."

"Of which you're the exception."

Kix took the opportunity he'd been waiting for and moved in, trapping her against the side of the truck before she could escape. He speared his fingers through the silk of her hair and turned her face up to his, delighting in the way her cheeks flushed with color and her eyes couldn't hide the fact that she wanted this as badly as he did. "Darlin', I can't let that insult to my manhood go unchallenged." He dipped his head and sealed her lips with his own.

Cady melted the moment his mouth covered hers. When his tongue teased her lips open and stroked inside, she felt like someone had poured warm honey into her.

The man could kiss. That didn't surprise Cady in the least—what did was the fact that she not only let him, but couldn't help returning the kiss. She wanted to eat him up.

Kix groaned in response and pulled her even tighter against him, thrusting his tongue in and out in a rhythm that had her cunt clenching and her nipples straining. Cady shivered and pressed closer. God, he should be banned or jailed—everything about him was sinful and tempting.

He shifted again, burrowing his cock closer to where it wanted to be. Damn, but this attraction had him feeling like a bull rider who got tossed and stomped on right out of the chute. If he didn't get a tighter hold on himself, he was going to end up hog-tied and too sorry-assed in love to care.

They were both breathing hard by the time the kiss ended. Cady somehow managed to move away from him, her eyes once again dropping to the erection that pressed boldly against his faded jeans.

Kix grinned. He was randy as a stud and lighthearted to boot. "You're a mighty fine distraction, little darlin'."

"I do have a name," Cady muttered.

Kix pulled her against his body, tight enough so that his heavy cock pressed against her. She shivered in response. His answering laugh was low and husky as he whispered a kiss along her neck before nuzzling her ear.

"Oh, I plan on using your name all right, Cady, just like I plan on hearing you scream mine."

About the author:

Jory has been writing since childhood and has never outgrown being a daydreamer. When she's not hunched over her computer, lost in the muse and conjuring up new heroes and heroines, she can usually be found reading, riding her horses, or hiking with her dogs.

Jory welcomes mail from readers. You can write to her c/o Ellora's Cave Publishing at 1056 Home Avenue, Akron OH 44310-3502.

Why an electronic book?

We live in the Information Age—an exciting time in the history of human civilization in which technology rules supreme and continues to progress in leaps and bounds every minute of every hour of every day. For a multitude of reasons, more and more avid literary fans are opting to purchase e-books instead of paperbacks. The question to those not yet initiated to the world of electronic reading is simply: *why?*

1. *Price.* An electronic title at Ellora's Cave Publishing and Cerridwen Press runs anywhere from 40-75% less than the cover price of the <u>exact same title</u> in paperback format. Why? Cold mathematics. It is less expensive to publish an e-book than it is to publish a paperback, so the savings are passed along to the consumer.

2. *Space.* Running out of room to house your paperback books? That is one worry you will never have with electronic novels. For a low one-time cost, you can purchase a handheld computer designed specifically for e-reading purposes. Many e-readers are larger than the average handheld, giving you plenty of screen room. Better yet, hundreds of titles can be stored within your new library—a single microchip. (Please note that Ellora's Cave and Cerridwen Press does not endorse any specific brands. You can check our website at www.ellorascave.com or

www.cerridwenpress.com for customer recommendations we make available to new consumers.)

3. *Mobility.* Because your new library now consists of only a microchip, your entire cache of books can be taken with you wherever you go.

4. *Personal preferences are accounted for.* Are the words you are currently reading too small? Too large? Too...**ANNOYING**? Paperback books cannot be modified according to personal preferences, but e-books can.

5. *Instant gratification.* Is it the middle of the night and all the bookstores are closed? Are you tired of waiting days—sometimes weeks—for online and offline bookstores to ship the novels you bought? Ellora's Cave Publishing sells instantaneous downloads 24 hours a day, 7 days a week, 365 days a year. Our e-book delivery system is 100% automated, meaning your order is filled as soon as you pay for it.

Those are a few of the top reasons why electronic novels are displacing paperbacks for many an avid reader. As always, Ellora's Cave and Cerridwen Press welcomes your questions and comments. We invite you to email us at service@ellorascave.com, service@cerridwenpress.com or write to us directly at: 1056 Home Ave. Akron OH 44310-3502.

NEED A MORE EXCITING
WAY TO PLAN YOUR DAY?

ELLORA'S
CAVEMEN
2006 CALENDAR

COMING THIS FALL

THE
ELLORA'S CAVE
LIBRARY

Stay up to date with Ellora's Cave Titles
in Print with our Quarterly Catalog.

TO RECIEVE A CATALOG,
SEND AN EMAIL WITH YOUR NAME
AND MAILING ADDRESS TO:

CATALOG@ELLORASCAVE.COM

OR SEND A LETTER OR POSTCARD
WITH YOUR MAILING ADDRESS TO:

CATALOG REQUEST
C/O ELLORA'S CAVE PUBLISHING, INC.
1337 COMMERCE DRIVE #13
STOW, OH 44224

Discover for yourself why readers can't get enough of the multiple award-winning publisher Ellora's Cave. Whether you prefer e-books or paperbacks, be sure to visit EC on the web at www.ellorascave.com for an erotic reading experience that will leave you breathless.

www.ellorascave.com